Cover design by: N.D.R
Library of Congress Control Number:
Printed in the United States of America

T0638869

Introduction

Hi, if you are hearing this, then that must mean we lost. What I am about to tell you may be hard to believe. Over 1,000,000 Americans have been reported infected and 67,000 have been reported dead. In the next few months 65,000,000 more people will die. I didn't believe it at first. Who wants to believe that there is a bigger plan in life, and we are not in control of it? After you hear my story, I hope that you will take this oppotunity to dig deeper. Don't take my word for it, and stop taking things at face valuable. They want us to be in denial, ignorant, and to take them at their word. I wished I would have opened my eyes sooner rather than later. Even though what I now know has cost me my life, it's a noble death. I would rather die fighting than to live my last days sleep walking.

January 1, 2020 I was given the opportunity to work for Billionaire Farmsworth of Farmsworth Enterprises in Chicago. My Granddad and his Granddad were old friends. He gave me a job working for his Investigative Reporter John Blackmen as a personal assistant. Mr. Farmsworth owned the "Chicago Streets Newspaper." My dream was to become an Investigative Reporter for the "Chicago Streets Newspaper."

January 15, 2020, I went to see my Granddad at his Senior Living Residence on the North side of Chicago. I
was nervous about my first day as a personal assistant. This job was my chance to show them that I hadwhat it took to be a reporter. I didn't want it to seem like I couldn't handle the pressure even as an assistant.

"Hey, John John," my Grand Dad yelled out the top floor of his window. He always knew when I was just about to walk up to the

door. I go inside and he has a plate of food for me. "Eat up son, and put some meat on your bone, my Granddad said with a smile. So, Granddad, what's going on in the senior living world?
Granddad: Well, have a seat John. I must tell you something, but it can't leave this room. You must promise me that you will keep this with you." I promise Granddad. What's going on? Is everything ok? You're not dying, are you? You're dying, aren't you? No!!!!!!

Grand Dad: No, son, I am not dying. A long time ago I was very naïve and ambitious. I wanted to be the king of the world, and no one could tell me what to do. Robert Farmsworth, I, and a few others made a promise to rise to the top at all cost. The world is a very dark place if you continue to walk through it with your eyes closed. I was young and didn't know what I was getting myself into," my Granddad cried out with a devastating look on his face.

What are you talking about Grand Dad? Are you in so type of financial debt? Do you have a gambling problem? Whatever it is Granddad, we will get through this. We are a team. There isn't anything in this world that we can't happen. So, what is it Granddad?
Ring....Ring...Ring

"Son there something you must know," my Grandad continued to repeat. I reached for my phone and its Robert Farmsworth. Hello Mr. Farmsworth. How are you doing today sir?

Mr. Farmsworth: Hello John, I wanted to check in with you before you start your first day of work. Are you excited to be working for the number one newspaper in the world, said Mr. Farmsworth?

Yes, I am Sir. I am very excited. Thank you for this opportunity. I promise I will not let you down. I will show you that you that I am a dedicated and a hardworking person. My goal is to become an Investigative Reporter.

Mr. Farmsworth: I am sure you will do a phenomenal job. Your parents would have been proud of you. I went to school with your parents, and we became good friends. I know that they are smiling at the person that you have become. Is your Granddad with you?"

Yes, he is. Do you want to talk to him?

Mr. Farmsworth: Yes, if it's not too much trouble. I would really like to get his opinion on something. You, know he helped build this company with my father?

Yes, we were just talking about the good ole days. Hold on, I will put him on.

Granddad, its Mr. Farmsworth, he wants to talk to you.

Granddad: John, I need to talk to you when I am finished talking with him, ok?"

Yes, Granddad I am at your disposal.

Mr. Farmsworth: Hello John, so how long has it been?"

Granddad: Not long enough. So, what do you want? If you are wondering if I told him anyone, then I haven't said a word. I am no longer in, but I know the rules.

Farmsworth: You know there's not an out, but it's good to know we have your support. We don't need the truth getting out. People wouldn't understand what we are trying to do.

Grand Dad: So, you think this is good for the world? What you we started and continue to do only benefits us. This is not for the people, it's for the people in power.

Mr. Farmsworth: So, I see you got rid of all your electronics? You know that we wouldn't want you to think that we are trying to babysit you. We don't spy on one of our own unless it is deemed necessary."

Grand Dad: Do you know what your father asked me before he passed away?

Mr. Farmsworth: My old man grew soft in his dying days. He wanted us to pull the plug on something he helped create. He knew as well as I did that, it no one can stop this organizatoin from getting what they want. The world that we live in has the strong and the weak. You are either going to survive as one of the strong, or parish like one of the weak. So, whatever you are thinking about doing don't do it. You may not care about your life but think about Lil Johnny.

Granddad: Goodbye, Robert Farmsworth.

What's wrong Granddad? You look like you just received the worse news in the world. I couldn't help but hear that you were a part of something crazy in the past. What was so bad that could affect the world?

Grandad, whatever it is just tell me. You are freaking me out! My Granddad looked so worried. I didn't know what to think or do at this point. It had to be something serious for him to change his demeanor so quickly. I just hope I am ready to face what's coming.

Granddad: Let's go for a ride son. I think I want some ice cream. Don't you want some ice cream son? Yeah, let's go get some ice cream. I know just the place to get it. I will drive.

Ok, Grand Dad.

So, he drove, and he drove. It seemed like we were in the car forever. We ended up going out of the city, and near a corn field with no stores for miles. I started to realize at that moment, he had something life changing to tell me.

Grand Dad, why are we out here? I don't think you wanted any ice cream judging by where we are now. So, what's going on???

Grand Dad: There is an organization that started centuries ago. Some people called it a secret society, some may call it a cult, and others may think that they worship the devil. Whatever you may want to call it, it they have plans for the world as it always has. But this time what they have planned has grown even bigger than I could have ever imagined. It can't be stopped, but at least I could make sure you're ok.

There are people out there that feels the need to cleanse the earth, and to make it great again. They want the world what it once was. A world free from over- population, diseases, poverty, and death. This group believes that the world is coming to an end. The time has come once again for them to stop the disease from destroying what's left of the world.

Grand Dad, who are these people, and what are they planning? How can we stop them? Are you apart of this?

Grand Dad: I was a part of this group a long time ago. I was naïve back then. I thought I could help make the world a better place. They feed me hopes and dreams. I believed in what they were telling me, and I didn't realize until years later what I had gotten myself into. I walked away from that life, and never looked back.

So, is that why Mr. Farmsworth needed to talk to you? He wanted you to help them destroy the world. What have you gotten me involved in Granddad?

Grandad: Robert Farmsworth is just one of many apart of this organization. He just wanted to make sure that I continue to follow the rule even though I am no longer with them.
What are your rules? So, are you done with them, or are you lying to me? Why didn't you say anything about this to me before? I must walk into his company tomorrow knowing that he is trying to help destroy the world.

Grandad: I am sorry John, but we don't have that much time left. They are planning the cleansing soon. It will be reported from one country to the next until it spreads all over the world. The media, health officials, and the general public will help the virus spread without them even lifting a finger.

Grand Dad: Ceo, Moguls, and the rich will sell their stocks until it's over. The media will report whatever they tell them. Misinformation will be the new truth. It will spread so rapidly by the time anyone catches on it will be too late. Everything they wanted to be done will be done. All, I want is to make sure you have a fighting chance. Even though I am not in my family and I are protected. The only rule is you can't tell anyone about this. I know you have a finance and kids. When the time comes you, all will be taken to a secret location until this all passes.

So, I am just supposed to keep my mouth shut? You know I can't stand by and watch millions of people die. How, could you even ask me to do that? Why is this happening? We need to go to the police, the government, or someone that could help us!!!

Granddad: It is not that simple son. This group has their hands in every single organization on this planet. I was you once. I wanted to save the world, but we are not in position to fight them back. So, please go to work, and just be ready when the time comes. Don't try to be a hero or rock the boat. Just do what they ask of you, and nothing more. If you follow these rules, then son you will be just fine.

I will keep my mouth shut, but this not right. May God have mercy on their souls. Can we go back now? I must get home. Tiffany and your grandkids are waiting for me.

Grand Dad: Sure, of course John. This doesn't go beyond us. As, I stated before when the time comes you all will be take care of. Failure to adhere to these rules will put us all in jeopardy. Do you understand me my son?

Yes, I understand, Granddad. I will just go to work and keep my head down. You have always been there for us. After my parents were murdered, it was you that took me in. Everything I am now is because of what you taught me. So, I trust you, and I will keep my mouth shut.

Grand Dad: When we get back in the car, we never had this conversation. We will not speak a word of this again until the time comes.

How will I know when the time comes? What are they planning on doing?

Grand Dad: Since, the beginning of time we have had plagues, diseases, famine, wars, and natural disasters? Some events as happened due to no control of our own. However, most diseases and disasters have been created by man. Every time something threatens our way of life, then it must be destroyed. We are responsible for Influenza, the Bird Flu, Mad Cow Disease, Ebola, the Corona Virus, and many others.

Grand Dad: This time we are calling it the Mors-20 Virus, which is Latin for Death. They are calling it "The Cleansing (The Beginning of the End). Nothing, or no one can stop it. They will create mass hysteria, offer a cure, and offer solutions. You will be told to shelter-in–place, self-quarantine, stock up, and follow all the instructions that the media gives. During this time the organization will be selecting who they want to survive.

You just said we, Grandad. Are you still with them? Have you been lying to me?

Grand Dad: Sorry, son. I meant them. All, of this have made me a little bit crazy. I am no longer with them. Let, go home. On the way we can get some ice cream from Cold Stone. I know you love the "Got to have it" cake batter ice cream.

My Granddad and I gets the ice cream. We go back to his place and talk about the good time when my parents were alive. I leave and go home to my family. I sit on the couch to digest every bit of information my Granddad had given me. I don't know if I could keep everything in and keep it from the ones I love. It was a lot for one person to bare, and now I must carry this alone to keep them safe.

Its January 16, 2020, and it's my first day of work. I am so, excited to be working for the Chicago Street Newspaper. I see newspaper clipping of stories that received National and global attention over decades. It's so much talent and history in this room. Someone yelled out, "Hey, Kid over here. It was Mr. Blackmen the Lead Investigative Reporter for the Chicago Street Newspaper.

I calmly walk to his desk as he's touching a stress ball in the air. So, I take a sit next to him, and he's working on a story, and at that moment I realized I was hooked. No, matter what happens from here on out; I am here to stay.

Mr. Blackmen: Welcome to the best place to work. You are going to love it here. I have been here for over 20 years now. Come take a ride with me kid. We are on the job 24/7, and a story waits for no one. So, let's get going, shall we???

So, we head to the roof on the building. It high and we could see the top of all the buildings. We can see all of Chicago. Everyone looks so small and out of reach.

I thought we were chasing a lead or working on a story? Why are we on the roof? Don't we have a job to do?

Mr. Blackmen: Look kids; I brought you up here to tell you the truth. What you are about to hear is for your ears only. I will tell you what I told the other assistants I had who by the way didn't listen. This job will suck the life out of you whether you want it to or not. It is up to you to decide whether you can take it. It will be more bad days, then good.

You will want to quit probably on day 3 or 4 of working here. You may or may not become a reporter.

So, are you telling me I should just quit, and walk away from all of this?

Mr. Blackmen: I am telling you to do what you want, but no that you have walked in already 5 steps behind. You are a young black man, and that's one strike. You are smart, determined, eager, kind, and hard working. Put all those things together and you are at a disadvantage.

Mr. Blackmen: Look at me, and tell me what do you see?

You are a successful black reporter for a well-known news-paper. You are well respected, and inspirational to people all around the world.

Mr. Blackmen: What I see when I look in the mirror is a man who came in wanting to be the difference for change. I wanted to save the world even if it was one person at a time. I wanted to help uplift my people, bridge the racial gap, and grow as a person.

So, you don't think you have done any of that? You are well respected, and because of you a lot of lives have changed for the better. I know it's not exactly as you wanted it to be, but you have done a lot of great this for this world.

Mr. Blackmen: Do, you believe in God?

Yes, I do, but what does this have to do what we are talking about?

Mr. Blackmen: So, you better get right with him now if you haven't already. We are living in dark days my friend. I have a feel-ing something big is about to happen, and it won't be by God. No, my friend what's about to come will be something a man made.

So, you know; did they tell you?

Mr. Blackmen: Tell me what? Who? Kid what are you talking about? Do you know something? Tell me what you know.

I don't know anything. I am just a little confused by all of this. So, what were you working on back at the office?

Mr. Blackmen: Well, the company wants me to do a fluff piece on Valentine's Day that's coming up in a few weeks. "What's your plans, and how to kick start a dying romance?"
So, I am guessing you're not going to do it?

Mr. Blackmen: Kid, I knew I liked you. No, I am not going to do that story. I am going to do a story on the effects of the 5 G cell towers all around Chicago. They are trying to expand them into neighborhoods area of low-income communities. Those towers generate radio frequencies that causes radiation, cancer, and could even damage DNA. They have them by landmarks now, but who's to say they will stop there. In other cities they are placing them near communities.
So, why aren't people speaking out against it?

Mr. Blackmen: People are speaking out against it, but the Media, and those in power are trying to bury it. So, it is up to people like us to get the truth out there by any means necessary.

Why, haven't you told your story? If you know the truth, why haven't you exposed them?

Mr. Blackmen: You, can't just run into a burning building without a game plan.

So, who do you think are those in power? Do, they have a name? What do you think they want from us?
Mr. Blackmen: You, ask a lot of questions kid. It's good to have questions but be careful what you say even around me. You can't trust anyone. I would even say don't take my word at face value.

We tend to put our trust in people. It's good to have a heart but remember sometimes the one you love are the ones holding the knife.

I finally made it home after my first day of work. My finance Tiffany got in a few minutes before I did. The kids are in their rooms doing their homework. I wanted to tell her what was going on. What if, this was my last day with her? All I could do was hug her close.

Tiffany: Sweetie, why are you hugging me so tight? I don't mine the love, but is everything ok? You haven't seemed ok since you came from Grand Dad's place. What's wrong? We don't have any secrets with each other. We tell each other everything, so what's going on?

My love, everything is ok . I am just nervous about this new job. You know how much I want to make a good impression. All I want is to make my parents proud. They would have wanted to see me become a reporter. When I was a kid you remember I use to run around with a note pad, pen, candy box I used for a tape recorder.

Tiffany: You know you got what it takes to make it. You are a very smart, determined, hardworking, and dedicated man. They will eventually see what I have always saw in you. Don't worry about what may come. Just continue to work hard and be thankful for what you do have.

I love you my Queen.

Tiffany: I love you to; my King.

Two week go by, and I get an all hands-on deck alert from the Newspaper. Mr. Blackmen calls me on the phone.

Ring...Ring...Ring

Hello, Mr. Blackmen I am on my way now. I just stopped to pick you up some coffee.

January 26, 2020

Mr. Blackmen: Kid, I need you to drop everything you have and get here now. Kobe Bryant just passed away. He was on his way to take his daughter, some of her teammates, parents, and the pilot to their basketball camp. People are already reporting it without all the information.

So, does that mean we lost the story. Because we aren't the first ones to get the story out.

Mr. Blackmen: I would rather be last and get it right. I don't care who released the story first. All I care about is what we put out there is factual. So, here's what I know. There helicopter carrying 9 people including Kobe crashed in Calabasas. There were heavy fog conditions at an estimated time of 9:45 am in California. Now, if you are his family do you really want misinformation being reported out there?

No, but doesn't the world have the right to know?
Mr. Blackmen: His, family has the right to have the facts reported first. Would you want someone saying that someone is dead, injured, or was on that helicopter and wasn't? People have already saying that since Lebron has passed Kobe in scoring the secret organization got rid of him.
What secret society is that? Is there really such a thing as a secret society?

Mr. Blackmen: If they a secret organization, then no one would really know if they existed. See, we have our conspiracy theories. Such as the All-Seeing Eye on the back of the dollar bill. How the rich gives up a love one to join this secret group. It is all bullshit if you ask me. Or, is it? What do you think Kid?

Well, I don't know what to think. If the secret organization do exit, then it's best that we stay out their way. I don't want to fight what I can't see.

Mr. Blackmen: Well, then the best way to fight something you can't see is to bring it into the light.

How do we do that?

Mr. Blackmen: So, we must think outside of the box. We have to read between the lines and look beyond the surface. The best kept secret is when it's right in front of you. Are you ready Kid?

Yes, I am ready, so where do we start.

Mr. Blackmen: Do, you see anything odd about the Newspaper?

They have the death of Kobe on the front page.

Mr. Blackmen: Look a little closer.
I see that they are testing a vaccine for the Mors-20 virus. What is that?

Mr. Blackmen: I don't know, but we are going to find out together.

I don't think we should be doing this; it's probably going to lead us into a dead-end.

Mr. Blackmen: Kid don't you want to be a reporter, and not just some guy known for picking up coffee for reporters? What's the problem Kid? Is there something going on that you would like to share with the rest of the class?

No, I don't but I feel like the two of us will be enough to take them down.

Mr Blackmen: Let's talk to the Chief and tell him our suggestions.

Do you think he will be on our side? Chief has a boss, and they may tell him to drop the story. I don't think he will go for it.

Mr. Blackmen: Oh, Debby Downer. Look we are going to ask him out of courtesy, but we are moving forward with the story. All he can say is no, but I am going to expose them for what they are. So, are you with me Kid?

Yeah, I am with you Sir.

So, we walk to the office of the Editor and Chief Edwards. He looks pissed off.

Knock...Knock...Knock

Editor and Chief Edwards: Come In. What the hell do you want Blackmen????

Mr. Blackmen: Chief, I have a story for you. No, we have a story that we think the people need to read.

Chief Edwards: I already have someone working on the Kobe article. What else could be more important than that right now?

Mr. Blackmen: I am referring to the Mors-20 Virus that is being tested at Rustlers Hospital as well as people who are coming out with cures mysteriously coming up dead.

Chief Edwards: You're John Sr. Grandson, aren't you? I remember when him, and your parents came in here with you. They said this is where the magic happened. Your Dad was an Activist and a very powerful man. It's sad what happened to your parents.
Yeah, its ok. I know that they are smiling down on me from Heaven.

Chief Edwards: So, Kid what you do think about all of this? Do you believe in these conspiracy theory crap?
Mr. Blackmen: I am meeting with some sources today that are going to blow the lid of this thing. Just watch and see Chief. Just watch and see.

Chief Edwards: Well, until you do that, I want the "Can You find Still Find True Love in 2020?" I want that article on my desk in 2 weeks.

We will have it in two weeks Chief.

Chief Edwards: I knew I like you Kid. Now, both of you get the hell out of my office.
We leave his office and walk into the parking garage. Mr. Blackmen and I are just sitting in his car.

Mr. Blackmen: Kid, I want you to think about if you are a leader, or if you are a follower. Are you part of the solution or are you part of the problem? I will see you tomorrow kid.

Mr. Blackmen day after day he sits at his desk with his eyes focused on the screen. contact. Two weeks go by and he hands Chief Edwards the Valentine's Day article as he requested.

I walk into the office that next day, and everyone in the office has their eyes focused on the President's press conference. One of the reporters asked the President about reports of a possible Mors-20 virus in China, and the possibility that someone with was able to bring the virus back to the United States. The President told the press that the virus was a hoax made up by the Democrats, and that no virus would be able to get passed his team of doctors.

The reporters asked why he dismantled the CDC and the team of scientist that could stop a pandemic from happening. The President repeated that it was a waste of money, and the local authorities could handle any crisis that came their way. President Dumpster believed that it was all Former President Ocean's fault.

Mr. Blackmen smiles and looks at me and walks over to me.

Mr. Blackmen: Walk with me Kid. Did I tell you or did I tell you? This has government conspiracy all over it. They are already leaked to the press that it's a virus created by China, so they will have someone to blame when it gets here. Do you know what happened to the reporter who wrote the article about the researcher being done at Rustler Hospital?

What happened to him?

Mr. Blackmen: He no longer works there. In fact, no one has seen or heard from him since he they printed that article. It's as if he vanished out of thin air. I will bet you lunch that my sources will confirm that this virus wasn't created by China. In fact, I will go in further to say that when this is all over we will have some believing that the government created this to depopulate the world, some will believe that it was to distract everyone from the 5 G cell towers being placed all around the world that causes cancer, and other will think it was the wrath of God.

What do you believe the truth is?

Mr. Blackmen: I believe that there's a little bit of truth in all of it. But, without fact all we have are conspiracy theories. Conspiracy theories are what they want because they will just live on forever. No, one will pay attention to the truth that starring them right in the face. Everyone will remember what they assumed the truth to be. Everyone will think it was the secret organization behind this, or God punishing us. At the end of the day the people in power will continue with their reign of terror while society blinding points fingers at the wrong person. See, the devil greatest trick was pretending he never existed. Now, they will do the same in plain sight.

Ring...Ring...Ring

Hello Granddad, is everything ok?

Granddad: You are being watched. You must make sure the truth never gets out, or you will be putting us all in danger. I know you have a caring heart, but are you willing to sacrifice the lives to save the rest of the world who's doomed to die?

Granddad right now isn't a good time. I will talk to you later.

Granddad: Son, wait!

I hang up the phone because I can't let millions die, so a few can live.

Ring..Ring...Ring

Granddad I will call you back.

Tiffany: It's your wife.

Is everything ok? What's wrong?

Tiffany: The hospital is on high alert, and they want all hands-on deck. Something is big is happening and I don't know what? I have a bad feeling about this.

What did you tell them?


Tiffany: They left me a voicemail, but I am about to call them back after I get off the phone with you. Honey, I took this job to save lives. So, whatever it is we will get through it together.

Don't go into work today. Just wait for me to come home. Can you do that for me?

Tiffany: Do you know what's going on? Is there something you're not telling me?

I will explain everything to do you in due time, but for now you just going to have to trust me. Can you do that for me? Don't answer your phone for anyone except me?

Tiffany: You're scaring me. What's going on?

My love, my Queen, my everything. Please nothing is wrong. I just want you to trust me ok. I will explain everything to you later. So, for now please just stay in the house, don't answer the door or the phone.

Tiffany: Ok, we will stay put here. When you get home, you are going to have to tell me what's going on.

I will. I love you.

Tiffany: I love you more.

I hang up the phone. Mr. Blackmen is on the phone with one of his sources.

Mr. Blackmen: Trouble in paradise Kid? We are going on a road trip Kid.

I told my wife that I would be home soon. She is a strong woman, but right now she doesn't know what's going on.

Mr. Blackmen: Neither do we, unless you know something, you're not telling me. Look Kid; I am on your side. I know I told you not to trust anyone but give me something here. We will not be able to stop this unless we are working together.

Well, the truth is...

Ring...Ring...Ring

Mr. Blackmen picks up his phone.

Mr. Blackmen: Hello Sir. How can I be of service to you?

Mr. Farmsworth: The paper needs all hands-on deck. We need reporters ensuring the public everything is ok. We can't let fear spread because it is going to make matters worse.

Mr. Blackmen: I am trying to give the people the truth and let them decide.

Mr. Farmsworth: No, one knows exactly what the truth is. This virus came out of nowhere. As, far as we know this could just be a hoax. Until we have all the facts all I want you to do is to ensure that we are keeping the public calm. So, can I count on your support?

Mr. Blackmen: Yes, Sir you can count on my support.

Mr. Farmsworth: Tell John, I said he's doing a great job. We are glad to have him aboard. His parents would be so proud of him. Tell him that I would love to see the wife and kids when this is all over.

Mr. Blackmen: Will do, Sir. Bye.

Mr. Farmsworth: Bye

Mr. Blackmen hangs up the phone and looks at me.

Mr. Blackmen: He wants us to stop. We must keep going until the end. Are you with me Kid?

Yes, I am with you all the way.

Mr. Blackmen: Oh, by the way, he wanted me to tell you that he's proud of you. He also wants to get together with you and your family when this is all over.

Why would he say that?

Mr. Blackmen: Yes, it's seemed weird to me. I know he has a history with your family. But it just seems like a crazy time to be saying it. Don't you think?

Yeah, it does seem weird, but everything about this seems weird. He hired you to report the facts, and to let the world know what's going on. We are there voice, their eyes and ears. If we lie to them, then we are no better than the people who are causing all of this.

Mr. Blackmen: Before I was interrupted by the Boss there's something that you should know before going forward. I just received confirmation from my source who is by the way is going off the grid as we speak. So, I will not be able to contact him anymore. He told me that this was a collective agreement among nations in this group who released this virus into the world. Why do you think so many diseases, viruses, and bacteria mysteriously appear into the world out of nowhere?
This group created them for personal gain.
Mr. Blackmen: Kid, it's bigger than that. See, this virus my source says is about cleansing the world. This group wants more than half of the population in the world gone. They want to hit the edit button and take out parts of the world they don't want. This is a global extermination. He sent my files of conversations, emails, pictures, and all the proof I need to end this once and for all.
So, where do we start?
Mr. Blackmen: I can't go back to the office, and I am don't think

I should try to upload the files from home.

Do, you have a place in mind?

We could go to my church; they have a computer that we could use.

Mr. Blackmen: Ok, Kid let's do this.

So, I drive to The Chicago Baptist Church of Faith on the West side of Chicago. I hope Pastor Thomas is there. We arrive at the church, and Pastor Thomas who has one of the well-known, and well-respected churches in the world. The Former President and his family frequently visited this church. We walk inside the church and Pastor Thomas is sweeping by the first pew.

Pastor: Hello, John, it's so good to see you. How may I help you and your friend?

Mr. Blackmen: We would like to use your computer?

Pastor: Of course, it's in the back, and it's the first door on your right.

Mr. Blackmen: Leaves and heads to the back.

Pastor: By the look on your face you have a lot on your mind. Do, you want to talk about what's going on my son?

No, I don't think I can. We appreciate you letting us use your computer, but I don't want to put anyone else in danger.

Pastor: You, know your parents, grandparents, and their parents all came to this church. Even after your Granddad became a powerful man, he still was never above the Lord. See, he still came to church every Sunday up until your parents was called home. You want to call my parents being murdered called home, then go right ahead. They were murdered, and the person that confessed hung himself the fight night in prison. Now, I am starting to think he didn't do it. I don't know what I believe anymore. Secret organizations, virus, and depopulation, 5 G towers, and all this bullshit!!!!

Pastor: Do, you still believe in God my son?

Yes, I do believe in God.

Pastor: I am not talking about that every Sunday or when I am down on my luck faith. I am asking you to do you read the bible, get on my knees every day, and thank the Lord for waking me up in the morning faith.  See, there are those that say, they believe when they need something.  There are also those who believe during the good and the bad days that God is always with him. I am not telling you that you must be a bible carrying member or get the Holy Ghost. All, I am trying to tell you if you believe, then believe. You can't have one foot in faith and the other in doubt.

You are right Pastor, and I am sorry for not coming back after my parent's death. After their death my faith in God was lost. I always wanted to know if he loved us, then why do he let bad people live. Why did he let my good parents die, and that evil man live? I don't care that he killed himself later. He made his choice but didn't give my parents a choice  Free will is bullshit.

Pastor: Language my son. Language. We are in the house of the Lord.

Sorry, Pastor. I have been through a lot over the last few weeks.

Pastor: You, know whatever you say to me will be confidential.

Well, my Grandad told me....

Mr. Blackmen yells from the back room.

Mr. Blackmen: Kid!!!!!!!!!!!

I walk into the office in the back with the Pastor. What did you find?

Mr. Blackmen: My source sent me all the information on how, when and why it was all started. The virus was created here in the states, but all the major countries had a hand in it. Every major country was sharing their research of the virus with one another. When the virus was finally manufactured into was smuggled out of the countries and distributed to each country. They injected into a host, and now fast forward it today.

But there aren't any confirmed cases other than the one that was assumed to have come from China. Even the President believes it to be a host. No, media outlets have talked about it being a major issue.

Mr. Blackmen: Have you checked your messages on your phone yet. It's already spreading as we speak. They have started the extermination of humanity.

Pastor: So, this group you are referring to is trying to end the world? They are playing God. "Creator has granted us an amazing privilege. He has made us our children's educators, protectors, and counselors. The sheer magnitude of this responsibility can lead us to think we should be "like God" when it comes to them."

What are you trying to say Pastor?

Pastor: Ezekiel 18:20 - "The soul who sins shall die. The son shall not suffer for the iniquity of the father, nor the father suffer for the iniquity of the son. The righteousness of the righteous shall be upon himself, and the wickedness of the wicked shall be upon himself."

Mr. Blackmen: Pastor, with all due respect. The power that be doesn't care what God has planned for them. All, they care about now is making sure that until they burn in hell, they will destroy those that doesn't share their interest.

Pastor: In the book of Revelations – Revelation 5:1-14 "Then I saw in the right hand of him who as seated on the throne a scroll written within and on the back, sealed with seven seals. And I saw a strong angel proclaiming with a loud voice, "Who is worthy to open the scroll and break its seals?" And on one in heaven or on earth or under the earth was able to open the scroll or to look into it, and I began to weep loudly because no one was found worthy to open the scroll or to look into it. And one of the elders said to me, "Weep no more; behold the Lion of the tribe of Judah, the Root of David, has conquered, so that he an open the scroll and its seven seals."

I have someone to tell the both of you. Before I could utter another word my phone rings.

Ring...Ring...Ring...

Hello Granddad, is everything ok?

Granddad: You need to come home right now. It's starting. We need to leave the city now. Where are you?

Granddad, I am working right now. I will be home shortly.

Granddad: I am with Tiffany and the girls. I will just stay here with them until you get here. We can all leave together. Just remember what I told you son, and everything will be fine.

Mr. Blackmen: What do you have to tell us Kid?

Pastor: Whatever it is my son, you can tell us. Your secret will never leave this room.

Before I could say it a picture of this secret organization appeared on the computer screen. My Grandfather, Mr. Farmsworth Sr., and 10 other people were on this photo

Mr. Blackmen: This photo had to be over 20 years old. My Grandfather and Mr. Farmsworth Sr had to be my father age in this picture. As he searched from the file to file, we saw pictures of men and women in robes. Bio terrorism, nuclear weapons, starting wars, and the list goes on. Their targets are the homeless, minorities, the elderly, and any threat that threatens their power. Their goal is to cleanse the earth in 3 months.

Alert...Alert...Alert

We all look at our phones. The United States has just declared Martial Law. Every city in America is on lockdown. Then like a domino it continued. Every country in the world has now quarantine themselves off from the rest of the world. There are sirens going off. Helicopters are flying over our heads as we speak. You can hear gun shots going off outside.

Mr. Blackmen: I have downloaded and uploaded all of this onto a server at a remote site that they will never find. If, I do not make it in 72 hours this will go live on all social media site. Kid I am going to give you a copy of all this information just in case I don't make it through this. Your Granddad was or is a part of this. So, I get it. I understand why you seemed to be reluctant to help. But you must decide whether you are a part of the problem, or apart of the solution.

Pastor: So, what was it you were going to tell us? We need to hear it from you son.

A few weeks ago, my Granddad told me that he was a part of a secret organization that was planning on depopulating the world. They believed that the earth is too crowded, and that we were destroying it. They wanted to keep us from destroying us. They have been doing this for centuries and there isn't a way to stop them. This organization has their hands in everything, so the only thing to do is to stay out their way. My Granddad promised me if I stayed quiet that my family would be safe. He's no longer with this group, but we are safe because of all that he has done for them.

Mr. Blackmen: So, do you really think that your Granddad is not a part of this? Kid open your eyes and see the truth. Your Granddad never left this group. Once you are in, it's a lifetime commitment. These files show that they start implementing putting chips inside of people who receive the cure. Just, look at some of our world leaders,

Mr. Blackmen: Jim Carson the Artificial Intelligence Giant, Rap Moguls, celebrities, and the list goes on and on. They will be in the news for trying to build a monopoly, invest in pharmaceutical companies. All they are doing is rebranding themselves to look like an angel when they are really a demon. We have been receiving year after year nothing but propaganda to keep us from seeing what has been right in front of us the entire time. They have been going all around the world not to save it, but to ensure their destruction.

Ring...Ring...Ring

Mr. Blackmen: Hello Sir, how are you doing this lovely afternoon?

Mr. Farmsworth: Where are you and John at? I need you both to come to the office now!

Mr. Blackmen: Well, I can't do that Sir. I am working from home. When I heard the sirens and receive the alert I went straight home. They have declared Martial Law. There are tanks and National Guard patrolling the streets as we speak. Our essential personal are allowed outside.

Mr. Farmsworth: I will give you and John authorization to work during all of this. The public needs to be reassured that everything is going to be ok. So, I need you and John to come back to the office now.

Mr. Blackmen: I never said John was still with me. John went back home. So, you will have to call him, and ask him to come in. I don't want to take him away from his family.

Mr. Farmsworth: I called his Granddad and he said he was working, so I assumed that he was with you. His Granddad is with John's wife and kids.

Mr. Blackmen: Well, I don't know where he is. I will try to call him and let him know that you want us to come into the office right away.

Mr. Farmsworth: Good. I will see you all shortly.

Mr. Blackmen: I am calling my boss.

Ring..Ring..Ring

Chief Edwards: What have you done? I told you to drop the story didn't I. You had to make waves didn't you. I can't stop what's coming. I suggest that you lay low until all of this blows over.

Mr. Blackmen: What are you talking about? I was calling you because Mr. Farmsworth said all hands-on deck, and he wants us all to come into the office now.

Chief Edwards: Is, are you talking on a secure line? Did you get the phone I sent you?

Mr. Blackmen: Yes, Chief this is the phone you gave me for Christmas.

Chief Edwards: The office is closed. If you aren't essential personal, then you are not allowed on the streets unless it's to go to the grocery store. Even then they are only allowing you out for a short period of time. They are even talking about starting to do food drops. This is about to get worse before it gets better. You are not a part of their problem, and you don't want to know what they want the solution to be.

Mr. Blackmen: We are so close boss. I have all of the evidence to blow the lid off this secret organization. The proof that I have will expose them all.

Chief Edwards: Then what? What you think will happen when you attempt to expose them. I said attempt because who in their right minds are willing to risk their lives to go up against them. You don't think other people and groups have tried. Look I know you want to save the world and be the hero. This is one battle that you are not going to win.

Mr. Blackmen: I can't let them get away with this. They are going to have to answer to the people for this. If I let them do this million will die. I can't live with that.

Chief Edwards: Let's just say you do get this out there and you tell the world. Let me take it even further. By doing this you can stop them from killing millions of people. You save the world, and you put them in jail for their crimes.

Mr. Blackmen: That is the plan, but you don't think that will happen, do you? We can bring them to their knees. They need to be destroyed once and for all. This is bigger than you or me. If we don't stop them now, it will be the end of the world as we know it. I can't stand by and let this happen.

Chief Edwards, this is John. I know that you don't know me that well. But we there must be something we can do. This can't be how it all ends. Are we going to let them do this to us?

Chief Edwards: Are you guys by a tv? Turn on to the news. It doesn't matter what station. Turn it on and turn it all the way up.

Pastor: I have a tv in the corner over there. I will turn it on.

Pastor turns on the tv and onto the news. He turns the tv all the way up so Chief Edwards and all of us could hear it.

Channel Zero new: Dr. Phauci of the CDC, "It is sad that in the African American community there is a disproportionate when it comes to how the Mor-20 virus affects them due to asthma, obesity, diabetes, and high blood pressure. There is nothing we could do for them now but make it as comfortable as possible through this tough time. I will now let the President speak.

Hello, my fellow American this is your President Dumpster. I have acted quickly. I believe quicker than any other President before me. I take this matter very seriously more than I can say previous administration has ever done. We are developing a vaccine that will stop this virus that I from the beginning knew how serious it was. When the Democrats thought it was a hoax. I told my team that this was real and acted fast. The numbers are bad and will get worse. But we acted so fast that we will stop this thing.
President Dumpster: I will have to say in 3 months tops, hey maybe even sooner than that. They have a new cure called Hydroxychlorquine that would be administered along with a chip implanted inside so we can keep track of the process the vaccine

is making to combat the virus in the affected person. We are calling it the Hydro 2.0 cure. I think it's cool. Jim Carson and I came up with this name. I am sure no other President could have made a vaccine this fast or came up with a cooler name. So, we are going to start testing it out in the much-needed community such as the African community who desperately need our help. Without this vaccine I think the numbers for them would be astronomical. So, this is benefitting them more than it has any other group, and I know they are very appreciative of what my team is doing. Thank you.

Chief Edwards: Now, turn it to another station.

Mr. Blackmen: Ok, I will try Coyote News

This is Coyote News: "The US total of the Mors-20 virus has surpassed every country in the world. Its death toll has risen of the past few weeks. What was first thought of as a hoax has become a nightmare. As the United States are unprepared. Hospitals Emergency rooms are full, people are being told to stay indoors and shelter in place. Martial Law is now in effect. The National Guard are patrolling the streets and people with the virus are being quarantine away from their love ones. If you have the virus as of now there is no cure to fight it. The death as of now is 11,000 and counting. It has been discovered that this virus was brought to the White House attention months ago, and in 2005 the former President warned the country to prepare for a pandemic that unfortunate has hit us hard today. May God has mercy on our souls."

Chief Edwards: Try another channel.

Mr. Blackmen: PNE NEWS: 3 people were shot today on the west side of Chicago today. There was an elder man who was killed, a 3-year-old shot, and mother who's in critical condition. Neighbors say that they heard yelling and someone killing their door in. They called the cops, but by the time they arrived at the home the elderly man was dead. When they asked them why they did it, "They said this is Chi Raq; it's not made for the weak." The neighbors said they wanted all of their food and supplies that they have stockpiled over the years just in case of situations like the Martial Law that in effect right now. It's a sad day when you are prepared for the worst but didn't think things could get even worse.

Mr. Blackmen: That's enough, so what's your point????

Chief Edwards: Do you see what's on the news. They don't have to do anything. We are spreading the virus for them. Every single drop of fear that is placed around the world is creating a ripple effect that will eventually become a tsunami that we will all drown from.

Chief Edwards:  Fear is a powerful weapon, and it's the deadest weapon man has ever created. Fear will keep you in the house, fear will keep you in compliance, fear will create chaos in the streets, fear will drive you turn on your love ones, and fear can even kill you.

Pastor: God, isn't happy about this, they will have to face his wrath. He will be their judge, jury, and executioner.

Chief Edwards: I don't disagree with that Pastor, but I don't the group behind this care about where they are going when they die. They are only concerned with wiping out the population now to create their New World Order.  In 2014 the Former President Ocean stated that we had to prepared for something like this. He said that we had to prepare for a pandemic that could come with symptom like the flu, Spanish flu, pneumonia, Influenza, and even a common cold. Two administrations said the time to act was now.

Chief Edwards: Now, fast forward it to 6 years later, and we are in a global crisis.

So, you think this President is part of this group? I thought we had more deaths with the other virus over the past 3 decades.

Chief Edwards: Yes, but you must understand this group does what it wants when it wants to. No, matter how good of a person you are, they know that you have a breaking point. Each person in power has either gave them what they asked or didn't live to fight another day. They may ask them to not stand in their way or be the face to calm the people of their country down. Whatever they are told to do, it will get done either way.

Mr. Blackmen: I refuse to believe that the world is going to end like this. I am not going to just sit here and wait for them to kill me. I am not going out without a fight!!!

I am with you Sir.

Pastor: I am with you as well!

Chief Edwards: They will be coming for you all if they haven't located where you are already. I have said too much. They have satellites that can pick up what you are saying through your phone, computers, and any electronic devices with a microphone. You all are probably

being watched through your computer's camera.

Pastor: No, this building was built off the blood sweat and tears of my ancestors. They made sure that this building was protected from enemies far and near. I also took the liberty over the years in investing in equipment that will shield my building from being detected. This church doesn't show up on a map, my computer is on a secure server, and once you enter this building it is shielded off from the outside. If someone tries to trace your call or locate where we are it will say that we are somewhere overseas. Don't let this cloth fool you. I am a tech nerd first above all else.

Ring...Ring..Ring

It my wife. What do I say?

Hello my love. I need you and the girls to go to your Dads.

Tiffany: Hey, my King. I just wanted to let you know that I dropped the kids off to my Dads.

I thought you were with Granddad.

Tiffany: He, said he was on his way to meet up with you.

So, the girls are with your father, so, where are you?

Tiffany: Something doesn't feel right Love. So, I am headed to the place where you first proposed to me. Do you remember where that is?

Yes, I do, but what happened to make you feel this way?

Tiffany: I love you my King. I am proud of you and all that you do. I know that you parents are smiling down on you from Heaven. I am with you all the way my love. I must go. I will see you soon.

I love you too.

Pastor: I don't think you should go see your Granddad. If he is still about of this group, then this may be a setup.

I don't think my Granddad would set me up, he's not like that. The man he was isn't the man he is today. I know him, and I know he wouldn't do anything to harm us.

Mr. Blackmen: Then, why did your wife & kids leave him. If they were some place safe, then why leave? Your wife had to get a bad feeling, or sense something wrong. Your Granddad is still much a part of this as he was before. His name comes up a lot in these documents. He has a lot of blood on his hands.

Ring...Ring..Ring

Hello Grandad, I am on my way.

Granddad: Let me come to you. Where are you?

I am on my way now. I will let you know when I am close. I will see you soon.

Granddad: I will be here. Bye for now.

Chief Edwards: I think you should know the truth Kid. In order to get into this secret society, you must sacrifice a love one. You must give the life of a love one to them as a show of divine obedience to them. Robert Farmsworth Sr. Killed his wife to get in, Robert Farmsworth Jr. Killed his father to get in.

No, that can't be. He killed my parents to get into this organization.

Chief Edwards: I am sorry Kid. I have something to play for you. Robert Farmsworth Sr. gave it to me before he died. He knew his son was planning on killing him. So, on his death bed he told me everything,

Chief Edwards: He also gave me a tape recording on your parents before they died. I guess they knew something was wrong, and that they felt they had to make a tape for you. I haven't listened to it, but if you want, I can play it for you now.

You can play it for me.

John I: Hi, son this is your Dad. If you are listening to this, we are no longer with you. Now, you must listen to me. Your Grandfather is a part of group that wants to make the world in their image. This group sacrifices the ones they love. They wanted us to sacrifice you and we said no. So, I think that they are going to kill your mother and I for disobeying them. I think they are going to have my father do their dirty work. I love you son. I am sent you to live with your mother's brother, so I know you grew up to be a great man. If you happen to reconnect with my Dad stay far away from him as possible. Nothing good could come from being with him. I love you son.

Mary: Hello, my sweet prince. I remember when you took your first step, I wanted to pick you up. But you got right back up and walked to me. I could still hear your laughter, see your smile, and feel your warm kissed on my cheek. You are my world and know that this was the hardest thing I ever had to do. Don't live your life in fear but remember the world will try to tear you down.

Get back up and keep fighting. We have an estate that your Grandfather doesn't know about. There's cash, plenty of room for a family, off the grid, and secure. My brother has it for you when you are ready. Just tell him I miss my Mom and he will know what to do. I don't want to leave our son John.

John: Its ok my Queen. Son know that we love you. We are right there with you. Give them hell son.

Mary: Goodbye my sweet Prince.

Chief Edwards: Sorry, Kid.

Mr. Blackmen: If you are going to go, then record it. But I am heading into a dead zone where my signal doesn't even work. I am surprised I had service in her, and they couldn't track me.

Pastor: Well, I have the latest tech that can jam any signal, traces, or hacks. Nothing come in or out unless I want it to. That is why so many people feel safe coming here. They know that this place is off limits. Besides no one would ever expect a Pastor to be trying to go up against a powerhouse.

I think my Granddad will know if I am wearing a wire. I will be ok. I will see what he wants and meet back here.

Mr. Blackmen: I don't think we should meet back here. We will find you. They may try to have you followed once you leave him.

I tell you what take my phone and if I am not back in 3 hours have my wife call my Uncle. I want you all to go to the place my parents left me

Until this blow over.

Chief Edwards: Sure, thing Kid. We will see you there.

Pastor: How would you know where to go if you don't call him. I memorized all the numbers in my phone, and addresses.

I will just go to his house to get it.

Pastor: Just go down to the basement. Take these keys. I have a car with tinted windows and diplomatic plates. They will not stop you. So, use it to get out, but ditch it before you get to your Grandad. You don't want him knowing that you suspect anything.

Thank you I will. I will see you all soon.

So, I had down to the basement that looks like a car dealership. I push the button on the keyless remote, and it's a G6 with diplomatic plates. The garage door opens, and I drive right by the National Guard. I get a few blocks away from my Granddad and I walk the rest of the way.

I see my Dad standing looking at the city of Chicago Skyline. Is this a monster or my Granddad? Maybe they have always been the same person, and I just didn't realize it until now. What do I say to him? What do I do if he tries to kill me?

Grandad: I was beginning to think you wasn't going to show up. We must go get the cure now. I have a place for us to go. I have already taken your wife and kids there. They are waiting for us to comeback.

Granddad so much is happening. I don't know what to do. I didn't think that it would happen so fast. The National Guard are on every street corner. People are being forced back into the house. It feels like I am watching an end of the world movie.

Granddad: It's just going to get even worse son. Hospitals across America are overcrowded. They only want essential personal working. The news has already started reporting that Blacks are the most affected race in America. Caskets and body bags will be showing up to

Granddad: Hospitals faster than they can treat the patients. Half of the patients getting them will be told to the media to be Black. If the patients are treated or die of a preexisting condition, they are told to put down cause Mors-20. You can go in for a common cold and you will leave thinking you have Mors-20. This virus isn't going anywhere, it's just going to grow until they get them to give them what they want.

What do they want? They already have the world filled with fear. They are destroying families, causing panic, and crippling our society. What more do they want???

They want a New World Order son. I told you think was going to happen. This will not stop until the Blacks, poor, homeless, elderly, Mexicans, the sick, and anyone else that threatens their reign of terror are all dead. Just come with me son, and we will be safe.

You know I can't do that. I think you are lying to me. Why don't you just tell me the truth? You are still with these people. Are you going to kill me just like you killed my parents? Are you going to sacrifice my life like you done theirs?

Grandad: I see you have been talking to the wrong people. Why couldn't you have just followed the rules? I told them that you would be perfect to join us, but you had to go ruin it. No, one wants to follow the rules anymore. First, I had to get rid of Robert earlier today, and now you.

You killed Robert Farmsworth? I thought he was a part of your secret organization?

He was the leader for the United States, but we have regained controlled of that as of now. His views have changed. He was getting reckless, and sloppy. So, my partner and I had to get rid of him and show the organization that we shared the same views as there's.

Why did you murder my parents? Didn't you love your son and his wife? What would possess a parent to kill their own child? You don't have a soul. You are a monster.

Granddad: Well, son your father was supposed to join the organization back then. However, he had to make the ultimate sacrifice. It was either sacrifice you or his wife. He would do neither. So, they couldn't let him live knowing the truth about us.

So, you were already a part of this group before they died? Who did you sacrifice to get in?

Granddad: Before I go any further, I think there's someone you should see. My love can you come here please?

Out of his car came a woman older, but a face I could never forget. It was my Grandmother. It's like seeing a ghost, or someone rising from the dead. How could this be; she has been dead for over 20 years.


Hello, my grandson. I know this may come as a shock to you, but what we are doing is for the survival of the world. Your people are destroying this planet. The poor, the hungry, the sick, the elderly, and all your minorities are like a disease spreading across this great land of ours. So, we need to cut the poison before it spread even more.

My people? They are your people too. So, you are doing all of this for money and power? You all are killing innocent people, and destroying this planet for what?

Grandmother: My poor, misguided, and naïve grandson. This was never about money. This has been planned even before you were born. Not you, me, or your Granddad would have been able to stop what is happening now. You are either with us, or against us.

Granddad: You, see my son this is our time on earth. You people had your chance and you wasted it. Look at what you do to your cities. They purposely put liquor stores, fast food restaurants, and drugs into

Granddad: Your communities just to give you all enough rope to hand yourselves. We don't even have to do too much now. With preexisting conditions, the virus is spreading faster in the Black communities than any other race. Sure, the numbers as not as high as reported, but no one cares about facts these days. The perception of the truth today is all that matters.

Grandmother: Look at your people. They can't even follow simple directions. Across America people are being told its Martial Law. People are being told to stay in their homes. Only essential personal should be out, and what are they doing? They are having house parties, roaming the streets, killing each other, and disobeying ever single order put into place to keep them safe. This is obviously what we want and planned on happening. But it would be sad if I cared.

I don't think that they planned on taking me with them unless, it was in a body bag. I started to feel a little dizzy and light head. My Grandad pulls out a gun and tells me to put into to my head.

Granddad: Son, take this gun. You either kill yourself, or I will kill your family. The choice is yours, but we are running out of time. Your Grandmother and I have a private plane to catch.

Grandmother: Its, nothing personal son. This was going to happen with or without your permission. See, we wanted you to join us initially, but you are more like my son than you would ever know.

So, who did you both have to kill to join this group? At least tell me that before you kill me.

Granddad: I will grant you your dying wish. Your mother and I had another child before your died. We sacrificed our baby girl, but we thought that we could past our legacy down with our next child.

Granddad: I killed our baby girl as a sacrifice to this organization and t pledge allegiance to this divine order. It was going great until your Grandmother started getting curious about how I was able to be so wealthy and powerful at a young age. She saw photos, documents, and people that I had trouble explaining as time went on.

Grandmother: So, they told Grandfather that either she dies or someone else that we loved. Your father was a proud man and becoming very powerful. Robert and your Dad were best friends. They were like brothers. So, one day we came to your Dad and told him about the organization. We told him that if he sacrificed you, then all would be forgiven. They were going to let all of us live if they just gave them you.

Granddad: Your parents died because of you.

Grandmother: My son and his wife are dead because of you! So, of course you Dad had to say no. We asked if we could babysit, but they took the child to his wife's family home. They must have known what we're planning because for years we couldn't find you.

Granddad: So, we devised a plan. We cut their break line in their car, and we had someone follow them to make sure it looked like a robbery gone bad. You didn't even attend the funeral.

Grandmother: We, knew that whoever had you wasn't going to bring you back to us. So, we waited and waited. The organization forgave your father's for telling me and welcomed me in with open arms. See, we were able to sacrifice your father, mother, and she had a child on the way. By the look on your face I guess, they must have left that part out.

Granddad: So, you must know that your wife and kids aren't with you. Don't worry we will find them. They will think you went crazy. Stop coughing?

Grandmother: What's wrong with him? Do you think he has the Mors-20?

Granddad: No, he can't have it. The virus is the cure. Stop coughing or I will shoot you where you stand. So, since you know the truth, then you know that your parents were gathering information to take us down. If you have that information, we will let your family live.

Why does it matter what I do now? I am as good as dead anyway. I don't have any documents, and if I did, I wouldn't give them to you. So, what does the 5 G Towers have to do with all of this?

Grandmother: Ok, I will tell you all you want to know, so you can take this to your grave. The 5 G Towers is like a light switch that turns off every person around the world off permanently. All we must do is insert the chip in them with the cure, and when we are ready the 5 G towers which is conveniently placed all around the world will do the rest.

Granddad: With the cure and the 5 G Towers there is nowhere in the world a person could possibly go that we wouldn't be able to kill them. If you get the shot you die, and if you don't will mysteriously die from the Mors-20 virus.

Grandmother: Yes, there will be quite a few who slips between the cracks. Some of your people and other people across the world will try to rise. People will have their conspiracy theories, assumptions, and educated guesses. But when the dusty settles everyone will go back to their way of life. We will have the world as we want it, and everyone will just follow blindly behind one another.

Granddad: See, with the 5 G towers we can pick and choose

who we want to live or die. The chip that will be implanted into everyone will track every single person in the world. It will have all your information and data that we need to determine if you are worthy to live in our new society.

Grandmother: Of course, it gives off radiation, flu like symptoms. It kills off the sick, elderly, and people with preexisting conditions first. However, we need the virus to depopulate the world at a faster rate. We are receiving some resistance from a few countries, but we have contingency plans for those who try to resist our new way of life.

Granddad: See, son Robert Farmsworth dead corpse is at your place along with bodies of a woman and two little girls. As, soon as we locate your family they will be murdered. You will take the fall for their deaths. So, no one will believe you. I will be shot you in the leg, and the media will report that you flee the scene of the crime. If they don't kill you on site, you will probably bleed to death. By the looks of it you may already be suffering from the effects of the virus or 5 G Tower radiation poison.

They shot me in the leg and picks up the gun that they gave me with a glove and drives away. I thought I could by me some time by showing

That I may can contracted the virus somehow. Instead of killing me they wanted to frame me for murder as I bled to death out in the middle of nowhere. I started to get a little dizzy, and I passed out.

I woke up, and I was in a bedroom with my leg wrapped up like someone has been nursing my wound. The door opens, and its Mr. Blackmen, the Pastor, and Chief Edwards. Where am I? How did you all find me?

Mr. Blackmen: Kid, you love asking questions, don't you? We

had you followed. See, I am not only an Investigative Reporter. We are Masons Kid, and we have been going up against these secret organizations for centuries. But we can't do it alone.

Pastor: Your Dad was a Mason, and your Mother was an Eastern star. They were working with us to bring your father organization down before he killed them. Is there anything you can tell us that you help stop them?

Well, my Grandmother is alive, and she was the one who killed my parents. The secret society called G.O.D.S found out that my Grandmother knew about them. My Grandfather was supposed to kill her, but they promised them a sacrifice. They promised the G.O.D.S me. However, my parents sent me away. So, the only alternative was killing my parents. My Granddad helped cover it up, but she killed them to show that she could be trusted. So, they gave her a sit at the table. They faked her death so she could find me. I think they knew that my parents had information on them. They wanted me to find it, so they could destroy it.

Chief Edwards: So, where are they now?

I don't know. They seemed like they were in a hurry to get away.

Mr. Blackmen: I just checked the news on my phone. I think we should turn on the tv.

They turn on the tv in my room.

Coyote News: After declaring Martial Law a few hours later a young reporter and grandson of highly respected John Smith Sr. Killed billionaire Rober Farmsworth, his wife and two daughters. They bodies were found in his downtown condo. When authorities arrived one of the officers got off a shot and wounded him in his right leg before he fled in a stolen car. He is said to be armed and dangerous. Authorities overheard him saying that he was infected, and he was going to spread it to as many people as possible.

Coyote News: The National Guard and the police are working together to bring him in dead or alive. They are urging everyone except essential personal to shelf in place and stay indoors until they receive the cure. The President is working with the CDC, health officials, and the pharmaceutical companies to coming out with a vaccine as early as Friday. They are assuring all Americans that; they will be able to return to some sense of normalcy no later than Monday. This could all be over folks in a few days, so let's just listen to the President and ride this thing out. I am Peter Stone with Coyote News. Stay safe people help is on the way.

Where is my wife and kids? I need to get to my wife and kids.

As, I tried to get out of bed Mr. Blackmen and the Pastor tried to hold me down while Chief Edwards talked to me.

Chief Edwards: Calm down Kid. Tiffany is an Ancient Protectors and she is somewhere safe. She has been working with us to take these people down even before the two of you got together. She is one of the main reasons why you stayed safe all these years. She was our eyes and ears. Your Granddad just called you out the blue to send time with you after all these years. He wanted to reunite with his Grandson. Tiffany along the Ancient Protectors, Ancient Stars, and some help from a few other organizations kept you all out of harm's way. So, they are safe. Use this phone to call her right now. Just hit "0" and the call will go straight to her.

I calmed down and Chief Edwards gave me the phone. I pressed "0" and it started ringing.

Ring...Ring...Ring

Tiffany: Hello, my Love.

Hello my Queen. Are you and the girls ok? Are you safe? Where are you?

Tiffany: Yes, to everything. I am sorry my love for not telling you the truth. I am sure you did the same to keep us safe. As, you must know now I am an Ancient Star. I was given a task a long time ago to keep you safe, but I never intended to fall in love with you. My instructions were to befriend you and keep you out of harm's way. That included keeping you away from your Grand-dad, who I knew just wanted to use you.

So, when we met, it was by accident? None of that matters now. All that matter is that you love me now. Where are you and the girls at. Let me come to you.

Tiffany: They are trying to frame you for murdering us, and Robert Farmsworth. If you or I come out into the open, they will kill us. It is too risky right now. Just lay low. We are on a secure line, so they can't trace this call. We are all safe where we are.

This is the government, so don't that have satellite and special equipment to locate us? They can hack our phones, tv's, laptops, and any other electronic devices. How do we know there not watching us or listening to our conversation now? They could be on their way to us as we speak!

Tiffany: I love you my King but trust us. We have powerful friends, and devices ourselves. They are just getting started, and it's just going to get worse from here. There plans will not stop because of a few bumps in the road. Did they tell you anything that might be useful?

They told me they go by the name G.O.D. S, which stands for God OF Divine Servitude. My Grandparents and these people believe they are doing God's will. By depopulating the earth, they believe they are saving it from total annihilation of humanity.

My Grandmother is still alive, and she killed my parents. They decided instead of killing me, they would frame me for murder to discredit me.

Tiffany: Even if we could prove to the world that you didn't murder Robert Farmsworth, they will never stop coming after you. I am sure that you Grandparents are laying low and planning their next move with the other members.

The 5 G towers are the key. If we could somewhere tear them all down, it would slow them done.

Tiffany: Yes, my love. We have a team in place all over the country ready to tear them all down all at the same time. Your girls are right here, they miss their Dad. Say, hi to your Daddy girls.

Lays: Hi, Daddy, I miss you. Mommie said that you can't see us right now because it's not safe. I am giving you a big kiss and hug right now Daddy.

I love your Mya my princess. Keep Mommie and Kiya safe for me Ok?

Laya: will Daddy. I love you.

Niya: Hi, Daddy this is me.

Hi, my little princess. Are you keeping Mommie and Mya safe?

Niya: Yeah, Daddy I am keeping them safe. You can count on me. When are you coming home Daddy?

Daddy must  work and when that work is over, I will be home ok. Until then look out for Mommie and Mya. Can you do that for me my little Princess?

Niya: Yes, Daddy. I love you.

Daddy I love you more. Now, give Mommie the phone.

Tiffany: Don't worry my King this too shall pass.

I know, but my heart aches without you. I miss your smile, your laugh, and hold you in my arms. My life isn't the same without you standing beside me.

Mr. Blackmen: Kids, we have a lot of work to do. She will be there tomorrow, so don't worry. You will have plenty of time to talk you her. For now, we need to make sure tonight's plan goes off perfectly. Because one mistake, and this will be the end of us all.

Where are we?

Pastor: This is your parents place. They left it to you. We used to have our meetings here when your parents were alive. You can't even find this place on Google maps, and it doesn't show up on any satellite as well. I have a few connections at the Pentagon, Nasa, and some of the world best hackers making sure what needs to stay hidden stays hidden.

Chief Edwards: We are going on a road trip. There are some powerful people that wants to talk to you. They will tell you everything you need to know, and how important you are to all of this.

Mr. Blackmen: You aren't afraid of flying, are you?

No, why?

Mr. Blackmen: We, are going to Africa.

I am wanted for murdering 3 people. I have a gunshot wound. My face has been plastered all the news. By now I am on every social media platform. When the facial recognition and towers, they have I will be spotted as soon as I step foot into the airport.

Pastor: Who, said anything about going to the airport. Look outside. Your parents pick this spot for a reason. It has enough land for a plane to land, and take off in. So, we will be leaving from here.

Who are we going to meet when we get there?

Mr. Blackmen: The President of the Ancient Protectors and

Ancient Stars, The President of Africa, and other world leaders. Our ride is here. Are you ready Kid?

Yes, I am ready. I get dressed and I head outside to the private jet. I step inside. There is a man who is surrounded by bodyguards. It's the Mentor.. I never saw him in person until today.

The Mentor: Hello, John, I am sure you have a thousand questions you would like to ask me. But before you do. Have a sit. We will a long flight ahead of us. You look just like your father. He was a great man. We didn't see eye to eye on some things, but I respected him a great deal.

You, knew my parents? So, you know what happened to them and why?

The Mentor: Yes, I afraid that your parents weren't part of your Grandparents plans. Your Grandfather and I grew up together on the West side of Chicago. He had so much ambition, heart, and leadership That man wanted to make the world a better place for his people. However, when he went off to Harvard, with Farmsworth Sr., they

The Mentor: Came back different.

What do you mean different? Weren't you all friends?

Your Grandfathers parents wanted him to go to private schools, so that is where he met Farmsworth, and his future wife. When, he came back from Harvard I knew he was different. He insisted that the high society didn't change him, and that he was going to make a difference.

Robert Farmsworth Sr, and John Smith Sr. Started F & S Enterprises of Chicago. It started off as just an idea. They wanted to hire people from the old block and poor communities. In the beginning they kept their word. It was like having Black wall street back. They had the news, best restaurants, technology, and a lot more right in the heart of the city. I was proud of them. I was with The Nation by the time they returned, but I was proud of my brothers. This company became a multi – billion-dollar business.

How did my Granddad end up in a senior living apartment? I knew he had money, but when he told me what happened I believed him? He made me believe that he gave it all up for her. The thought of walking into a company that she helped built was too much for him to bare. So, he told me he sold his share to Robert Farmsworth Jr.

The Mentor: Your father never left the organization and had to make you believe he did for you to him. He had a fake funeral just so you could take the fall for what's to come. However, you weren't supposed to make it this far. If your father would have sacrificed you back then, they would have waited for them to have another child before they killed them. Eventually they would have found out that they were a Ancient Protectors and an Ancient Star. They only found out when your Uncle got custody of you, and they tried to come get you in the middle of the night.

What happened?

The Mentor: Well, your Grandparents decided to send a team to kidnap you.

Why kidnap me? What could I have possibly down at the age of 2? I was just a baby. Were they really going to kill a 2-year-old?

The Mentor: Yes, they were going to kill you, but they were going to groom you into thinking you were a part of a bigger plan. They were going to teach you how to be one of them, and then when the smoked cleared you were going to be the one standing there with the murder weapon. You were going to be a sacrifice or made to be an escape goat. Since they couldn't use you as a sacrifice, then they were going to make you an escape goat.

So, what is so important that I needed to go to Africa. Why am I so important?

The Mentor: Well, my child, before Robert Farmsworth Sr, passed away he left all his shares to you. His son doesn't have any stock in the company. Robert Farmsworth had 50 percent. Your Granddad had 25 and he gave 25 to your father.

So, I own 75 percent of the company?

The Mentor: Yes, and a whole lot more. See, you own the patents to all the 5 G towers going up all around the world. You own satellites, tech companies, defense contracts, oil, diamonds, island, the chip the carries the vaccine and the list goes on. Your Grandfather and Robert Sr. Had their hands in every major business in the world. So, your death, or jail time would give all your shares back to your Grandfather making him the majority shareholder in the company.

So, why go to Africa, and not go public with all of this? I could just buy him out; couldn't I?

The Mentor: If, it was that simple, then we would have done it years ago. Besides they would never let you make it to the boardroom alive if they thought you would try to attempt to buy him out.

Couldn't the other members develop 5 G towers, or the things they need to depopulate the world?

The Mentor: Each member has a part in all of this, but America is the center piece of it all. If you take out America, then the other pieces would not be able to function. We stop your Grandparents, then we will at least set them back a few years.

Why are you looking at your watch Sir?

The Mentor: Because right about now the Towers all around the world are coming down. So, now they are going to have to rebuild them, and come up with a good reason for why it's necessary. See, during this chaos people are starting to see the truth.

We, just had to

The Mentor: Give our people a little push in the right direction. Pastor can you turn on the tv?

Pastor: Of course, my brother.

The Pastor turns on the tv:

World News: If you can see the images behind me, they are burning down the 5 G Towers. I am being told this is happening simultaneously all around the world. All the towers that has been built is coming down.  In Chicago they are spray painting Black Lives Matter on the side of the tower. I have reports that Africa, Korea, China, the UK, Italy, Russia, Canada, and many more countries are all tearing down the towers. Many believe that these towers are causing cancer, flu like systems, and the real virus killing people in this pandemic. This is Shaun O' Riley reporting you live from World News.

The Pastor shuts off the tv.

The Pastor: So, you see son, the revolution has been televised. However, the war has just begun.  We must walk into the valley of the shadow of death and fear no evil.

Mr. Blackmen:  Kid, you got this. I took this job because I thought I could change things once I got inside. I was doing a story about the good things that the church was doing. I met Pastor, and he told me about the Ancient Protectors. . So, I joined them, and continued to work undercover to gather as much information as I could against this company. We have been able to slow them down a little bit over the years, but it's like one you cut off one head another one takes its place.

They already have what they need to rebuild the towers, they have the chips, they have the virus, and they have the perfect fall guy in me when this is all over. So, how will we be able to stop them?

The Mentor: Now, that the towers are down, it will take them months to rebuild them. They will have to go to their plan b, and that is what we need to find out. They can't use the towers to active the chip that will kill off millions of people in an instant. So, they will have to come up with another solution and fast. We are going to Africa to get together with the other world leaders who are against opposing the new world order. Now, it's time to find out what their next step is.

After about 14 hours we arrived in Africa. We landed in Uganda at a base that couldn't be found on any map in the world. I wished I was coming here under different circumstances. Uganda looks amazing, and it's not the poor country America portray it out to be.

I enter a building that looks abandon, and when I step inside it looks like military base. They have guards everywhere, with computer screens monitoring activities all around the world. They have tv screens showing the towers coming down on the news all around the world.

The Mentor: Welcome to "The Mother Land." We have been coming her for centuries. To fight against those who choose to oppress us. Those that has used their privilege to destroy others not by the content of their actions, but by the color of their skin. The white man wants us to fold, the devil wants us to go away, and the powers that be wants to see their opposition to be exterminated. We are being pushed in a corner, and I refuse to hide in the shadows.

We enter the room and is like what you see on tv when Congress met. In this room there were delegates, world leaders, activities, and powerful people who wanted to see an end to this evil group hell bent on destroying the world.

President of Uganda: We are all here for one purpose, and that is to stop the secret organization known as the G.O.D.S from de-populating the world. They will stop at nothing to destroy my people of Africa. They will stop at nothing until all Africans are extinct. We must come

President of Uganda: together to stop their reign of terror once and for all. So, I will give the floor to The Minister who called this meeting bringing us all here today. You have the floor Minister.

The Mentor:  We might not all agree on what's best for our people, but something brought you here. Our skin color, the way we walk, talk, and live our lives may be different, but something brought you here today. You may not like me, or what to listen to what I have to say here today, but something brought you face to face with me. So, whatever your reason for being here we must come to a resolution before them devils make one for us.

Chinese Delegate: I am here for my people, but why should we help your people. It is your people who has brought that Mors-20 virus to China. Your people are attacking our people in America, so tell me Mentor why should I help your people.

Kenya Delegate: Your people in China has refused to serve Afri-cans in China. We want your people to leave Africa because it was your people who started this virus in the first place.

President of Uganda: We took our people from out of China because they were being mistreated. However, that's not why we are here today. We are here today to come up with a solution. Phi Yates is trying to push a chip that will carry the virus to depopu-late the world. Without the 5 G towers they will have to move to plan B.

Mr. Blackmen: I am representing America, so can anyone tell us what Plan B is? What's their plan since the towers are now des-troyed? What's the timeline for them destroying the world? We have them down, but not out. They will not stop until they have the world the way they want it to be. So, what's their plan, and how do we stop it?

South Korea Delegate: If, your President would have listened when he took office none of this would have happened. We had a team of expert years in advance preparing for moments like this. Your President dismantled the team of National Institute of Health Department, CDC, Scientist, and Health expert who could have pretend this from happening. At the very least your country could have been better prepared to stop this virus. Your President, your government and your fear gave them the powers to spread this disease. My country is fine, so why should we bother to save yours?

UK Delegate: I heard from a reliable source that Jim Carson has develop a vaccine that will be in a syringe with a chip inside. Since they can't use the 5 G Towers to track who they want to kill, they have developed another method. They will be using the satellites from every country and hacking it. On 3/26/2020 they will push the button to kill everyone who has the chips implanted inside of them.

This could all just be rumors. How do we know if your source is realiable?

UK Delegate: The 5 G towers where just a distraction and a way to help kill people in a 300 radius of the tower with the radiation faster. The towers gave off emitted enough radiation that it gave them the same systems as the virus. So, once people started to complain of being sick, they would just blame the phone industry for putting up the towers not the government.

Chief Edwards: I am also a Delegate for the United States. On October 18, 2019 experts simulated what it would be like to have a virus and back then it was called Coronavirus Pandemic, and it killed 65 million people. They sent a group of Public Health Experts to New York to do this simulation.

Chief Edwards: They wanted to see how businesses, governments, institutes overseas, and the world in general would react to a pandemic with a high risk of world ending repercussions in a what if scenario. They called this "Event 201" better known as CAPS: Coronavirus Associated Pulmonary Syndrome. They used Brazilian pigs that passed the virus to their farmers. The result was the had mid flu like symptoms of the likes of pneumonia. Fast forward it three months, the fake illness had 30,000 people sick and 2,000 dead.

Chief Edwards: The news that reported it is a mirror image of how the news are reporting this virus. When the scenario finally ended after 18 months there were 68 million people dead because of this virus. This is the same virus, but it has a different name. However, what the scenario, and the simulation doesn't show us is that it was man made. This virus was created by this organization to depopulate the world. People will go online and search for articles like this to fuel the fire to an endless list of conspiracy theories.

President of Canada: So, America knew about this. I respected your Potus 44, and those before him. I can't support the man that you all in the office today. You have over 26, 000 deaths, and 605, 0000 confirmed cases in the United States. More importantly, your country knew years in advance that this could happen. President after President warned the next President to prepare for a pandemic such as this. You even had a simulation months ago testing this disease itself under a different name. Your President is just as much to blame as this secret organization. He could have stood up against them as we have and stopped Phil Yates from creating this deadly virus chip implant.

Hello everyone, my name is John Smith Jr. Many of you may know my father John Smith II, and my Grandfather John Smith Sr. Right now my Grandfather and Grandmother have framed me for the murder of

Robert Farmsworth Jr., my wife, and kids. My wife and kids are alive and well. Robert Farmsworth is dead, and the police are looking for me. They wanted to use me a fall guy and give my Grandparents total control of F & S Enterprises. With total control they can continue to sell my patents, create even more deadly devices, and create a world where their kind our exist. I was told by my Grandparents that they are planning on killing off the sick, elderly, poor, homeless, minorities, and people who are a threat to their **New World Order.**

They called themselves **G.O.D.S**, but they are nothing more than just human beings that can be taken down. We can stop them if we work together. I may not be a Delegate, a President, an Activist, or anyone important. I am standing here before each one of you asking for you to stand with me.

Mr. Blackmen: They are using the Darwinian theory "Survival of the fittest." They think that they can select who lives and who dies. We are the prey, and they are the predators. We can't let them hunt us down. This is not the natural selection, and they were not biologically created to be superior to everyone else in the world.

Pastor: I not sure who all follows the word of God but in Isaiah 26:20, which is the same day as 3/26/20. "Go home people, and lock your doors, hide yourselves for a little while until the Lord's anger has passed." While they are trying to kill us; my Lord is trying to heal us. See we can look at this as the end of days, but I see this a time to rise my people. I see this as a time to come together as one. God will judge them when their time comes, but until then we need to come together to stop their reign of tyranny.

President of Uganda: So, any suggestions on how we stop this from happening? My people of Uganda will not allow anyone to come into people homes to give them the shot. Jim Carson is forbidden from to Africa.

President of Uganda: Coming back into our country. So, the real question is how we stop this virus from killing of the Americans?

President of Italy: I think it will get worse before it gets better. Even if we stop all contact from America my sources from America said they have a plan for that as well. Their Plan B is to effect as many people with the virus in America as they possibly can. When infected the carrier of the virus would be able to infect anyone, they encounter it. From my sources once they active the chip in everyone they are planning on sending out people all around the world. Once they have people in every country, it will spread like wildfire. We will not be able to contain it. We can stop planes from going out, boats, cars, but for how long. Someone will get in, they are connected to so many people.

President of Italy: They may even have a spy in this room. We do not know how deep this rabbit hole goes.

Delegate of Russia: This is true. There is no way of stopping them. Our President doesn't like your President, but even he knows the power of this group. You are either with them or you are against them. So, Russia doesn't stand a chance against this deadly virus. Even though they will be going after the Blacks first. It is apparently clear that those that doesn't bow to them will be eliminated as well.

The Mentor: They have my people running around like saves for pennies. They have them working dead end jobs knowing that the cost of living doesn't much their hour wages. They put liquor stores, fast food restaurants, churches, abandon buildings, drugs, guns, and no resources in their communities. They give us high blood pressure, hypertension, asthma, obesity, diabetes and cancer. We have been told there's nothing we can do for you. So, if you think for a second, I am going out without a fight you are sadly mistaken.

Japan Delegate: So, what do we do? Because all I have been hearing is what they are doing, and not what we can do to stop it. I had a chance to join this group, but I declined, but there were plenty of others ready to take my place. I met your Grandfather a very long time ago with Robert Sr. They were ambition then, and your Grandfather will stop at nothing to keep his seat at the table. This is his baby, and they will kill him if it fails. Your Grandfather has never failed.

What if we stop the implants from getting out? We can destroy the implants factory and get rid of every vaccine that they have. If we destroy the implants, we will stop them from injecting people on 3/26/20.

China Delegate: You, don't even know where they are holding this vaccine. They could have hundreds of thousands of warehouses all around the world with the implants. We don't even know where to start.

Kenya Delegate: I like the Kids, idea. We may not all agree with one another, but at least this kid is coming up with a solution. I am sorry for what your country has done to your people. I mean our people. I am in.

Iran Delegate: Your American President praised China over and over for containing the spread of this global pandemic. The head of the CDC is also an employee of Jim Carson who is a part of this society organization. So, you come here today to beg for our help when we know that this is a battle we cannot win?

France Delegate: My country has over 17 thousand death, and

it is because of you Americans this pandemic wasn't caught in time. In Wuhan where the first outbreak occurred was never contained. Your people funded a research of a simulated pandemic. If you and China wants to work together be my guess. We will continue to allow your country to use us when it's convenient for you.

Belgium Delegate: We have under five thousand deaths, and we have been able to contain the spread of the outbreak. Ever life that we lost is a devastating lost to our country. We are doing everything in our power to continue to help our people. We will do what we can to help our fellow countrymen.

Kenya Delegate: In all of Africa we only have 872 confirm death cases. So, why is Jim Carson, the CDC, and health officials anxious to start testing the vaccine on us first. They want to come here because we have natural resources, and we are one of the riches countries in the entire world. If they can destroy us, then they could just come in to take whatever is they want. So, yes, we will help you Americans, to stop them from setting foot on our land.

Uganda President: Let's adjourn this meeting and continue at the same time tomorrow. Everyone remember we are still on high alert, so don't leave the facility. Thank you.

So, everyone gets up, and heads to their rooms. I stay inside the room from a minute.

Mr. Blackmen: Are you coming Kid? We have a big day a head of us tomorrow.

Pastor: We, had a long flight, so it's best that we rest up.

Chief Edwards: Yeah, I am a little beat myself.

The Mentor: You did well John. Your parents would be proud of you. We have a long way to go. The road ahead will not be easy, but we all will get there together. Remember sacrifices will be made, and lives will be taken. However, a man who stand for anything; will fight for nothing.

Just give me a moment. I am ok.

So, as everyone leaves, I just look around the empty room. How did I get here? How did they world get here? People are dying all around the world, and for what? This global pandemic wants to wipe my people off the face of the earth and depopulate the earth because we threaten their way of life. God, please tell me what to do next.

I am laying in my bed in my private room on the base. I hear a knock on the door, and it's the Pastor.

Pastor: Get dressed my son. There has been some key intel that has come to the group's attention. We have a couple spies in our midst.

Wait what? How did spies get into this meeting?

Pastor: Just as well as we had spies infiltrated their organization, they have done the same to ours. We know when what their next move is and have a plan to stop them.

Pastor: They have them in a holding room in the basement. One of them asked for you personally.

Why would they want to talk to me?

Pastor: We are all about to find out. Everyone is waiting in the room for you to come.

We arrive in this viewing room, and there are two men sitting in the other room handcuffed to the floor with long chains. They have a table in front of them. The President of Uganda is standing by the control panel. Everyone else is sitting behind him.

President of Africa: Glad that you could join us. Doubt worry they couldn't send back any information or disclose our location.

See, I knew they may be someone in our group that couldn't be trusted. So, any electronic devices were deactivated by our satellites as soon as everyone landed. But, the question of the day is why have they aske for you.

South Korea: We, all know why they asked for him. He is just like his Grandfather; he is one of them. He cannot be trusted. Just through him in with the rest of them.

The Mentor:: This young man has nothing to do with them. Let hear what they have to say to him. This could all be a part of their plan to divide and conquer.

President of Uganda: The floor is yours Kid.

I step up to the control panel, and I push the button:

What do you guys want from me?

China Delegate: You remind me so much of your parents. Too bad, they were killed before your Grandparents plan was fulfilled.

You know nothing about my parents. You don't have the right to mention talk about them.

Russian Delegate: Blah, Blah, Blah. You Americans and your feelings. Are you people do is talk. You, think just because you have us as hostage that their plan will stop? The answer is no. We came here to simply give the kid a message.

Chinese Delegate: See, Kid you are not the only one full of surprises. Your Grandfather knew that one day if you lived through this, it would come a time where you would have to make a choice. So, if you chose the wrong side, then he would give you one more chance to change your mind.

Russian Delegate: Join us, and all will be forgiven. If, you continue down this path you will die right along with the rest of your people.

I don't know if you know this or not, but my Grandparents just tried to kill me. They have also framed me for murdering my boss, and family. So, why would they change their minds when I was their perfect escape goat?

Chinese: Your family will be safe, but the rest of the world no. You can't stop what's coming Kid. Do you really think stopping them from giving the vaccine will stop them from depopulating the world? They have backup plan after backup plan. This is just the beginning of the end for your country and all the other countries all around the world.

Russian Delegate: My group don't like your people Kid, and never have. We will mostly everything that has to do with your race, and whoever is left will have to accept our way of life. Africa you people have fought so hard to keep us out, but that's not going to work once this is over. Once we are done with you people, then we will have all the power in the world.

So, this is all about world domination and power?

Chinese Delegate: What is your answer Kid? Your time is running out. It is 9 am over her, so it is 5 pm in America. You have until midget in America to give your Grandfather an answer. If you don't give him an answer, then he will take that as a no. If, you say yes, then your life will be spared. You must go back to America with us.

Kenya Delegate: Why would we left you leave with him? The both of you will be convicted on treason, and rot underneath a jail cell for the rest of your lives.

Chinese Delegate: Where do you think we will be convicted? You will have to send us back to our home country. We will not see a day in jail. You can't stop the way that is coming. You people should have joined the cause when you had your chance. Trying to keep all of your resources from the rest of the world wasn't your best idea.

So, this is about seizing all of Africa's resources?

Russian Delegate: This is about seizing everyone resources. We are the New World Order. The G.O.D.S will reign down upon men and strike their hearts with fear. They will bow upon our feet and ask for our forgiveness. For we are superior to all, and the weak shall be self-servant to those above them.

Chinese Delegate: Enough questions. Give us an answer by midnight or suffer the fate with your people.

I turn off the speaker button, and I turn around to face the group.

So, what's the plan? Are we still going to go after the vaccine?

Chief Edwards: I think we should grill them some more and see what else they know. They said that they have multiple plans, and we can stop what's coming? I think we deserve to know what would happen if we stopped the vaccine from being shipped out.

Mr. Blackmen: So, let's go asked them a few more questions.

UK Delegate: I think we should continue to get information out of them. Right now, we have no leads to where the vaccines are, or where they are headed.

I go back to the control panel, and I push the speaker button to talk to the spies.

Can you tell us where they stored the vaccines?

Silence...

Can you tell us where they stored the vaccines? Say something please!!!

Russian Delegate: You Americans are amusing. You pick a tv host for a President. You thought having a Black man before him who be your way to get to your people to the Promise Land. You people are a joke. Your country is a joke. I can't see how you all lasted this long. Without our interference your country would probably be at the bottom of the ocean. We say jump and your country say yes Sir.

Chinese Delegate: The Vaccine is in a Warehouse owned by Phi Gates back in America. It is in plain sight. In a few days it will be sent to every hospital around the world, military base, and Fema facility. They will have tents and camps set up for people who want the vaccines. Right as we speak, they are passing a bill to force the shot on anyone who refuses it. So, this will give them the right to go into everyone home starting with you Americans to give them the cure.

What do you mean starting with you Americans? Isn't this cure meant for the entire world? Don't they want to depopulate the world, and not just America?

Russian Delegate: You Americans are easily persuaded and fooled. You buy into the hype. It has already cost you people hundreds of millions of dollars to do the testing, and it will cost trillions of dollars for the vaccine. It was a brilliant plan by the organization if I do say so myself. Why, not make money while doing a little bit of Spring cleaning.

Why, tell us everything nothing that we can stop you all now? We can put an into all of this.

Chinese Delegate: Who, said we told you everything? As, we stated earlier this is one of many plans put into place. You stop one plan as you have already had, then another plan is set into motion. You, all are 5 steps behind us. This is just us having a little fun before the curtain opens.

Did everyone get that?

South Korea: So, the rest of us are safe? Why have we come here if the only country affected is America?

Russian Delegate: Who said that the Americans will be the only ones affected? Have fun you guys. The 26th is only a few days away. The clock is ticking. Tik Tok. Tik Tok. Tik Tok.

Chinese Delegate: You, should have said yes, so now you must suffer the consequences of your actions. You still have a few hours left. But I see that you are your father's son, and you will make the same mistake he did. So, now get ready to join him.

Russian Delegate: Now, run along kids; you guys don't have that much time left.

Before I could gather my thoughts to leave the room, I look up to see my family standing there. My wife Tiffany, Laya and Niya standing by the door. They ran to me, it felt like a dream.

I can't believe you all are here. How? Why?

Tiffany: I wanted to surprise you. So, much has been going on. I just wanted us all to be together. Besides, it's not safe for us in America right now.

Laya: Daddy we missed you so much.

Niya: : Daddy are you ok?

I am ok, and I missed you all as well. The only thing that matters is that we are all here together now. I must go back to America, and then I will come back for you all.

Tiffany: You all are planning to stop the distribution of the vaccine, are you?

How, did you know about the vaccine?

Tiffany: We knew that there were going to be distributing a vaccine, but we couldn't get an exact location. I am guessing you all have that now.

So, we leave the room, and head to the plan. The other Delegates stayed behind. It was the Minister, Mr. Blackmen, the Pastor, Chief Edwards, and I. It felt like the plan ride lasted forever. We landed in San Diego CA airport owned by the Ancient Protectors. The airport was a couple miles away from Jim Carson warehouse that was holding the vaccines.

They called in a team to meet us there to destroy the warehouse. The warehouse is heavily guarded. I don't know how the team is going to destroy it without people dying on our end. This is the moment that we have been waiting for. If, I must die so the rest of the world could live

Is a choice that I am willing to make.

They send in the soldiers who were ex-military and trained killers. One by one the guards of the warehouse went done. They plant the bombs around the facility.

BOOM...BOOM...BOOM!!!!

The building goes up in flames. There black SUV's coming out of one of the garages. The team shoots out the tires, and it's a shootout. Everyone except one guy is alive from the three SUV vehicles. They pull him out, and its Jim Carson.

There are sirens, and it sounds like they are getting close. All the vaccine is destroyed. There is nothing left of the warehouses except ashes. We all leave, and the team blindfolds Phi Yates. He is taken to a secret location, so we can find out if there is more. We are hoping this is a victory that will end it all, and that there isn't another plan in the works if this one failed.

We get to the site, and a Mom & Pop store. Why would they bring him here? This is out in the open, and people shop in this area. I hope they know what they are doing. As, we go inside, there is an elevator in the backroom. The elevator takes us to the basement, then seems to look like its underground. Its, a never-ending tunnel, and its heavily guarded as well. There are guards at every corner of this place. We arrive to this train and we get on, and it takes us to the end of the line.

As, we get off the train we all just stop and look at this place. This can't be real.

The Mentor: Welcome to the Nation son. This is one of many places I call home. Jim Carson is brought here, so we can get answers, and this is not the end. We must find out what it is that he knows, and what their next move will be. He is in the interrogation room right now. We will listen in.

We walk into this building much like the other interrogation room in Uganda., but a little bit smaller. It's a two-way mirror, and he cannot see us. He is tied to a chair; his eyes have cuts dripping with blood. His ribs are broken, and there are torturing tools on a table next to him.

The Mentor pushes a button on the wall and says tell us what you know.

Jim Carson: April 16, 2020 do you know what that is? Come on guys you all must know what that is. How about you Pastor? If anyone know what that means; I know you do?

It is when Passover ends. "Moses goes to the Pharaoh and asks that he let the Jews go free from Egypt. Each time the Pharoah says, "no," God sends a plague down on Egypt (darkness, lie, boils, cattle disease, etc.) The tenth and final plague is the most drastic: the killing of the first born by the so-called angel of death. In order to protet their first-born children, the Israelites marked their doors with lamb's blood so the angels of death would pass over them. Thus, the name Passover, which is "Pesach" in Hebrew. The Israelites were ultimately freed from slavery and wandered the desert for 40 years before making it to the promise land.

Jim Carson: I see you know your Bible Pastor. So, I am guessing you all are here. I hope you all enjoyed your small victory, which is going to be short lived. Mr. Blackmen, Chief Edwards, The Minister, and John Smith Jr; is that everyone? The moral of the story is that we are G.O.D.S, and we are here to set you all free. You all are slaves to this world, and don't belong here.

Chief Edwards: So, you knew we were going to try to destroy the vaccine? Was this all a part of your master plan?

Jim Carson: Why, do you think we want to do this? Yes, we want to depopulate the world. But, what do you think the real reason was? ` See, you people are so aggressive, and angry all the time. First, we made you all believe that you were immune, and you fell for it. Then we made you all believe that you all were the main group at risk. It was like a puppet show, and we just watched you dance as we pulled the strings.

Mr. Blackmen: You all are going to pay for this. We have all the evidence to take your group down. You all are done. When this story gets out you will be doing life in the Federal Prison. All the vaccine is destroyed. The towers are all down, and you have no way of putting the chip to destroy us inside of us now. So, why are you smiling?

Jim Carson: I am smiling because this isn't over. Why you all were chasing down the vaccine we were sitting back watching the world crumble. Look at the state of the world. People are pushing our narrative without us even saying a word. The economy is about to crash, people are dying, no one knows what to do, and then when the smoke clears who will they run to? I will tell you who they will run to; it will be us.

So, you want the world to come to you all for help? That's not going to happen. You are going to jail for life, and so are the rest of the people in your organization. I hope it was all worth it!

Jim Carson: Mr. John Smith Jr.  It's nice to finally meet you as an adult. I remember you were just a child.  Your Dad brought you to your Grandfathers office the day before his death. We were literally discussing how we were going to kill him right before he walked in. Talk about awkward timing.

Shut the hell up!!!! You have no right talking about my father at all. Don't ever mention his name again. Do you hear me???

Jim Carson: Yes, I hear you loud and clear. You are so much like him. If you would have only listened to your Grandfather, we could have put all of this on someone else. They initial planned to make Robert Farmsworth death a suicide and used him as the mastermind behind this virus. When the group found out you couldn't keep your mouth shut; we decided that you had to go. Soon as you step foot back out into the real world you will be arrest by the authorities. Everything that has happen will be on you. Everything you all have done was for nothing.

The Mentor: Since the vaccines have all been destroyed; what is your next move? Was the warehouse that we destroyed the only place holding the vaccine?  Did we destroy the vaccine or was it move to another location?

Jim Carson: You all destroyed a prototype of a vaccine that were testing. We have warehouses all around the world with manmade viruses, vaccines, and the blueprints to put up more towers. As, we speak we are developing even more towers to be installed.

Pastor: So, what are you all planning?

Jim Carson: We have no plan? The plan was to put fear into everyone and everything. You turn to the media, family, friends, and love one what do they all have in common? They all are producing fear for us.

Pastor: Fear will not win. We have the Almighty God on our side.

Jim Carson: Yes, you do, but what about the millions and millions that let their fear take control? You can't save them all Pastor, and fear will do our job for us. There are people giving false information and adding fuel to the flame. Soon, the entire world will be so afraid to think for themselves. We will be the voice of reason.

Mr. Blackmen: People are already Woke, and aware of the lies. No, one believes in the propaganda that you are infecting the world with. So, tell us the truth!!!

Jim Carson: You, want the truth? Have you been watching the news? I am one of the wealthiest men in the world. I have done humanitarian aids, fight for human rights, and help fund cures for a multitude of disease. Yes, there are some who are aware of my true intentions. For, the most part due to my propaganda I have been able to come off as a man of the people. Your President is telling the public to inject themselves with disinfectant. So, tell me if the world is willing to do that, then may God help you people.

Pastor: You are nothing more than a devil worshipper, and a fake. God will judge you when your time comes. Until then you will spend the rest of your days in jail.

Jim Carson: Actually, I won't be spending any time in anyone's jail. I am going to walk out of here unharmed. Just go back to your lives, and when the time comes, we may give you all some mercy due to that fact that you all had the balls to go up against us.

The Mentor: We will not negotiate with the devil. You will leave when we are ready for you to leave. Under this we are at war, and I will protect my people at all cost. So, Jim Carson you are under no condition to be giving demands.

Jim Carson: Do, you know who I had to sacrifice to join the G.O.D.S? When I did it, I didn't feel any remorse. I knew at that moment that I was cut from a different cloth. I knew at that moment I was destine for to do the Lords work. My mother gave birth to me, but it was only fitting that I was the one to give her back to the Lord.

You are a sick fuck!!!! How could you kill your own mother? What is wrong with you???

Jim Carson: What you call sick; I call enlightenment. My mother gave herself to the cause willingly. We walked into the sacred circle as an offering to the G.O.D.S and her last gift to her son. She knew the meaning of true love and sacrifice. What have you people sacrificed other than each other lives. Your communities are in shambles, crime is at an all-time high, and even the virus can't make you people act civilized.

The Mentor: : What is the next phase? What are they planning next? If you don't answer, then we will continue with the interrogation. Trust me you haven't felt the worst of it yet.

Jim Carson: As, much as I have enjoyed your hospitality; I am going to have to decline your offer. There is no next phase. The phase is fear. Fear is what is fueling this pandemic, and fear is what is going to be your people's demise. Look we don't have to do anything but watch you people destroy one another. There are already people protesting the lockdown with assault rifles, purge mask on, and comparing it to the civil rights moments. You just got to love America and it's thought process. You give a mouse a crumb of cheese, and he will bring his friends back for more. Now, everyone is fighting over freedom that they never had. Got to love the irony.

Mr. Blackmen: What's so funny about what's going on?

Jim Carson: In a few weeks this country will continue to ramp up the numbers of death from this virus. The American people will suffer the most causing their debt to increase, and then their worst fears will set in. The country is already divided, and this will bridge an even wider gap. State after state will reopen without a game plan causing the fear of the pandemic to spread. Even the States that are going to stay on lockdown will not be able to keep those that choose to stay open out. Talks of vaccines, implants, and the cure will flood social media. Fema camps will be placed in every single town in the United States. People will fight back creating even more of a panic. Your people will fight against hate groups, and their own people. Cities will be burned to the ground out of rebellion. Riots will spill out into every community not protected by us. These people blood will be on your hands. If you would have just let us do our job, it would have been over.

If, this was your plan all along, then how have we caused any problems? We have essentially helped you guys accelerate the fear by making everyone think it was a virus. So, tell me then why people are dying if there isn't a real virus out there.

Jim Carson: : I never said there wasn't something out there. In every disaster, plague, pandemic, epidemic there has always been a man-made virus. Yes, we put a virus out there, and it's like the flu. If you take the proper precautions it is treatable. However, overtime we made it strong enough not to be able to fight off if you have preexisting conditions.

Chief Edwards: Where are the rest of the vaccine, towers, and implants housed at? Where is your headquarters located? Who are all the members of the organization? We want names.

Jim Carson: Well, the vaccines, towers, and implants are housed on a need to know basis. I don't need to know, so I can't tell you where they are. As, far as where we are located. We are located nowhere. Everyone communicates through video chat on a secure server. I don't know who all is about of this group because it is constantly growing. To keep everyone honest some members identities are kept secret.

The Mentor turns on the Tv in the room and turns up the volume so Jim Carson could hear it. Jim Carson is at the White House briefing with the President of the United States. How can he be at two places at once if this briefing is being broadcasted live?

The Mentor: Something was brought to my attention while you were talking. You were right about one thing the Media will have a role in all of this. Isn't that you Jim Carson the Software Mogul and the man who is supposed to be a part of this untouchable group? So, why do they have someone pretending to be you at the White House?

Jim Carson: That can't be real. You had to have someone make a fake news conference to make me believe that my people turned against me. This isn't real. I have dedicated everything to them; they would never betray me.

The Mentor: Well, it looks like you have been replaced. The question now is what you are going to do about it. Because I have a feeling once we let you go, then they will come after you. You will be killed and replaced by the guy at the White House. Unless you want to be killed along with the rest of us; then you must give us something.

Jim Carson: They don't tell me much. I am helping them push for the H20 Vaccine for the Mor-20 virus and trying to get the cure out within 18 months. But, in order to do that we have to fuel the fire with fear. Fear is causing this wildfire to spread. If it spread far enough it will cause a war within each state causing a collapse from within. By pushing you all over the edge in 18 months you all will be begging for a cure.

So, there isn't another phase, or virus out there?

Jim Carson: We are the virus? Our own fear is the virus that's spreading around the world. America is the only country that is has so much hatred for one another that they can't see the truth right in front of them. If everyone would just believing every-thing, we tell them, then maybe you all would have a chance at survival. They will not stop until most if not all of you are dead. The Blacks, poor, minorities, and anyone that poses a threat are going to be dead. You thought this was bad wait until the second wave comes next winter. Your people pretend to be Woke, but they are just sleep walking.

So, when are the new towers going up? How close are they to finishing a vaccine? Are you planning on putting implants inside of us?

Jim Carson: Some of the towers are already being put back up, and as for the vaccine there are over 82 being tested as we speak. The implants will come when we announce to the world that we have a vaccine that will destroy the virus. The pandemic will go away for a few months giving you people a false sense of security. When winter returns so will the second wave of the virus with a vengeance. This time around no one will be able to stop it without the cure. The man-made virus will come in two parts. First it will be in the second wave of the virus, and in the cure to assure that we have depopulation. I need for you guys to expose them, so I can get my life back.

Mr. Blackmen: So, now you want our help? I thought you said that there was no way we could win? Why should we help you? You are part of the problem, and you want all our people to die.

Jim Carson: I can help you guys. I know how they think, and where they are holding the testing sites for the vaccines. All I need is for you guys to help me stay alive long enough to get my life back.

The Mentor: So, how is it possible for them to have someone who looks like you replace you? Is he a clone, your twin; what is he?

Jim Carson: When we joined, we gave them a sample of our DNA, and for decades we have been trying to perfect cloning. We only use it when people that we need don't follow the rules. If they need to be seen, then we will replace them with a clone. But I have done everything that they asked of me.

They have turned their backs on you. You are all alone now.

Jim Carson: They must think they I have been compromised and doesn't want to take any chances. On April 18, 2021 they will begin using the testing kits and reporting the changes in the rate the virus has affected each state.

So, tell us the truth. What's going on?

Jim Carson: : However, if you paid attention the CDC was looking for candidates last November to help with the Mor-20 virus testing. So, your President just failed to mention due to our coaching that this virus existed some time ago. When they do start the testing keep in mind that no one is trained for this, so the percentage of errors are high. The higher the mistakes the better the outcome is for them.

What is my Grandparents planning?

Jim Carson:: Well, since you now know that your Grandmother is alive, they are planning on creating chaos that no one will ever be able to recover from. It has already begun. The conspiracy theories are already out there, people are already afraid, and with misinformation no one is informed of what's really going on. One misinformed person isn't a problem, now try getting through to millions of misinformed people who ae now paranoid.

They threw him in a cell, gave him food and water. I don't think he would have shown us any compassion. It is April 16th, and the death toll is at 40, 0000 reported, and over 645, 000 people infected by the virus. I don't know want to believe any more. People are dying, some are recovering, and others fears are increasing with paranoia mounting right behind it all.

Chief Edwards: Let's see what's going on in the Media

Chief Edwards turns on the tv as we all sit at the table to eat breakfast in the Mentor secret hideout.

World News: It is April 16th, and the spread of the virus is increasing, but the President plans on reopening some states in the next feel days. This is earlier than initially reported for May 1st. He will be giving the Governors total authority to open some business to help people get back to some sense of normalcy.

Mr. Blackmen: The country isn't ready to reopen yet. This is just another trick by the G.O.D.S. We need to have a talk with Phil Yates. I think he isn't telling us everything.

Chief Edwards: Does, it even matter at this point. Maybe he's right and their isn't a way to stop them. Look Kid I joined the Masons to help our people and stop groups like this from destroying our people. I am getting old and tired. I am not the young fighter I once were. Sometimes you must know when to throw in the towel.

Mr. Blackmen: Chief you are the one who brought me into this organization. Do you remember what you told me?

Chief Edwards: Yes, but times have changed, and so have we.

Mr. Blackmen: You, told me no matter what happens over time never forget why you are here. We all have a purpose in life, and once you find yours don't give it up without a fight.

Chief Edwards: I am not giving up. I am just being rational.

We all head to the interrogation veiwing room, and Jim Carson is in the other room. He is on speaker so everyone could hear him.

Jim Carson:: Good morning everyone. What did I do to deserve all your presence this fine morning?

Mr. Blackmen: Cut, the bullshit. Why is President trying to end the lockdown so soon? I thought you said it would take months for a vaccine and that they wanted fear to set in to create even more chaos.

Jim Carson: Even though he works for us; we can't control every single word he says. Sometimes you just must let him loose, so far, he has worked in our favor. If he opens back up the states too early, then it will just create havoc among the people of that state. If they see a decline, it will just triple when the second wave comes. If they see increase in the infected, it will just create even more fear.

I have been doing some research of my own on you, and secret cults. You are mixed up in witchcraft, sex trafficking, being a pedophile, sacrifices, and the devil, and genocide. So, why should we help you, and get you back to your normal life. You are a horrible person.

Jim Carson: My way of life doesn't have to make sense to you. I am chosen by the G.O.D.S and for that I am worthy of divine praise. These people that you say I have hurt willingly gave themselves to me. You wouldn't understand.

Pastor: So, make us understand? Why do you feel that God has chosen you to prey upon the innocence? You don't think that is the devil in disguise my son?

Jim Carson: Save your prayers and your God for the weak. I am still a G.O.D.S, and when I get out, they will welcome me back with open arms. However, until then we can work together to stop what's coming. Then, we can go our separate ways.

The Mentor: So, you will just forget my secret location, all our faces, and everything we talked about? You have emails talking about pizza as it refers to children, you have pictures of yourself with your friends smearing animal blood on yourself. We had some of our best hackers hack your email addresses. So, tell me again why we need you.

Jim Carson: How were you able to... Oh, you took my fingerprints while I was drugged, and logged into my account on my phone. From there it must have been easy to download all my files. While the ones that they allow you all to have. Don't you realize those are the files that they wanted you to have. If I expose them, then they will have allowed all of secrets come to light.

Soon as you tried to access encrypted files, they thought I turned on them. You all are the reason why I was replaced. Look, if you don't destroy the phone soon, they will be able to locate where I am. You won't be able to block this location forever especially if you keep using my phone.

The Mentor: Don't worry about us. Your phone is already destroyed. The day you came her we took all he information off it, then we destroyed it. They tried to trace our location, but we had them thinking we were someone in Israel. The stuff that we have found on your phone has incriminating evidence for a lot of power people. You have celebrities, singers, rappers, ex-presidents, politicians, delegates, activist, and white supremacy groups, cults, and of course your secret organization. Most of it was infected with a virus, so we couldn't use it. But what we do know is that your people are of the devil. Mark my words we will stop you.

As, he stated April 16th Passover was over yet, our victory was short lived. It seems that things were just beginning. A couple days later they were testing people with containment kits that gave off inaccurate reading. So, no one knows how many people actual are infected, recovering from the virus, and have died from the virus. The NIH, CDC, and the health community are all scrambling for results by taking short cuts.

There are coffins out numbering hospital beds all cross America. People are going into the hospitals, but not all of them are coming out. They are reporting people with any pre-existing condition as Mors-20 patient. If you die of pneumonia, kidney failure, asthma, diabetes, or anything not related to the virus would be written down caused by the virus. Anything to raise the fear of the virus or downplay the virus the media has been playing the country like a violin. I don't blame all the media because it is up to us to question it. However, the more we question the more conspiracy theories surface. I am starting to wonder if Chief Edwards were right about this being a losing battle.

Mr.Blackmen: What's on your mind Kid?

I was just thinking about everything that's going on. What if we can't win this. When I go outside, I will be arrested, and will be convicted of multiple murders. Even if I could have my family come home, it would put all of them in harm's way. They will never let them come home to clear my name. I don't want to put them in any danger.

The Mentor: Your family is safe, and sound in Uganda. They put together a video showing that they are still alive and well. Proving that you didn't murder them, and that this were framed for them as well as Robert Farmsworth Jr. By showing that they are still alive will give them reason doubt that you murder Farmsworth. So, don't you worry about when you leave here. Just, think about what we need to do to stop them from killing off millions of people.

Pastor: We are all in this together Kid. No, matter what your background is, it all comes down to us working together to save the world. People don't know what's really going on, and they don't want to know. Most people like the idea of being Woke, and not knowing what's lurks in the shadows. Because facing the truth is depressing, painful, and will eat away at your soul. So, if you pretend as though it doesn't exist, but at the same time saying you Woke helps some people sleep at night. Denial is a powerful thing. It can help keep fear at bay, or it could be the very thing that causes fear to go over the deep end. Son, you are going to have to make a choice. Either you are part of the solution, or you are part of the problem.

The President are telling once again reminding the governors it is up to them to open their state, and some states are opening like Georgia. Chicago will reopen with restriction on May 1$^{st}$. However, there are people having parties, and showing total disregards to the lockdown precautions. The total number of deaths is America is 53,352, and only 1.57 % have been tested.

Ring..Ring..Ring...

It's my wife. Hello my Queen.

Tiffany: How are you my King?

I am good. I don't think we are done here yet. I have a bad feeling that there is more to this. They have replaced Phil Yates with a clone.

Tiffany: A few years ago, we got some intel that they had perfected cloning. They have been their technology to the highest bidder and using it to replace those that they need to control.

So, you knew about this? Why didn't you tell me?

Tiffany: I didn't know they would replace Phil Yates. All, I knew is that they have the resources to replace anyone by using their DNA.

Do you think they replaced my Grandparents?

Tiffany: I don't think so, he shares their vision.

Why didn't they use this technology to replace my parents?

Tiffany: Your parents weren't like them, and they knew that people would see that something was wrong. These clones can only follow orders and can't be the person that they were made to be. I wish I were with you. The girls and I miss you.

I miss you all too.

Tiffany: No, matter what happens from here on out remember that we will always be in this together. Ok, we are a team. We, rise and fall together my King.

Why are you talking like that my Love?

Tiffany: I have been talking to my organization, and they think something big is about to happen. Everyone is on high alert. I was instructed to stay put until further notice. I have prepared a video clearing your name for our murder. So, do what you need to do, and we will handle the rest. See you soon my Love.

See you soon my Queen.

She hangs up the phone and I just lay in bed. There is a knock at my door, and its Mr. Blackmen in a panic.

Mr. Blackmen: Phil Yates is gone and so is Chief Edwards.

What happened? How did he get out? Did he kidnap Chief Edwards?

Mr. Blackmen: I don't know Kid. Everyone is meeting in the surveillance room right now.

We all are in the surveillance room looking at the video to see Phil Yates escaped, and what happened to Chief Edwards.

The Mentor: At 3:30am Chief Edwards unlocks Jim Carson cell. With a gun in his hand he orders him to come out the cell. They go down to the garage and steals a car. They drive away at 3:55 am.

I thought those doors were remote operated. Why weren't the guards monitoring the cameras, and why didn't any alarms go off? How did he even gain access to a key or to the garage?

The Mentor: I let him go. Because you see Kid Jim Carson is a very sick man, and not because of what is planning. They think just because they have a lot of money, they can do whatever they want. About 20 years ago Chief Edwards daughter was brutally raped and murdered. It was by the one of one of the wealthiest families in the world. He said that she wanted it.

She was only 17 and he was 21. They found pictures of her partying, smoking weed, and made her look like a problem child. He got off scout free. No, jail time, or probation. Even when a video came out some time later of the rape, they said didn't we put the family through enough already. They buried the video, and no news company would touch it.

Was Jim Carson the guy who raped and killed her?

Mr.Blackmen: No, but he helped cover it up. He went to trial defending this family and painted them out as saints. Phil Yates doesn't remember or doesn't care.

What is he going to do with him?

The Mentor:: Since Jim Carson has already been replaced, then this one will probably be a casualty of war. He will kill him, but it won't bring his daughter back. The guy who did it died a few years later of a drug overdose. It wasn't in the papers or on social media. Everyone called pneumonia and said he has been fighting it for weeks before it took his life. So, I turned off the alarms, told the guys if Chief Edwards came to get the keys let him get them. This man needed this, so who was I to deprive him the justice that he seeks.

That wasn't justice that was vengeance.

The Mentor: Tell me John what would you have done if you were faced to face the man who help free your daughter killer? The man who rape and kill your family who didn't serve a day in jail. Would you turn the other cheek? Would you forgive him John, or would you make him pay?

Pastor: It's not that simple Mentor, and you know that. I remember when it happened because Chief Edwards came to me for guidance. We knew back then that we couldn't have done this alone. So, we joined the Ancient Protectors, and he started working for the News Paper. I ended up building my church from the ground up. We both served our communities together in different ways. Fighting the good fight against the powers that be.

So, now what do we do? We don't even know what they are planning next. Everything he told us could just have been a distraction or lies. What do we do now?

The Mentor: My men are prepared for the worst-case scenario. If they want to go to war, then we will go to war. We have satellites, hackers, spies, and powerful people behind us as well. Don't be fool by their scare tactics. When Chief Edwards is ready to come back he will.

I am about to go to my room. I am not feeling good.

Mr. Blackmen: Are you ok Kid? Just go lay down. Just relax, and come back in a few hours. Chief Edwards should be back by then. Who knows he might get some information out of the piece of shit before he's burning in hell.

I will be back in a few hours. Just going to lay down for a little bit.

I leave them alone in the surveillance room, and head to my room. All, I could think about is what was going through Chief Edwards mind right about now.

Jim Carson: So, where are we going?

Chief Edwards: Do you remember going to court about twenty years ago?

Jim Carson: I have been to court pretend of times over the years as an expert witness. Why, did I ruin one of your stories?

Chief Edwards: Do you know the Girberts?

Jim Carson: Yes, they are very close friends of mine. I grew up with their son Brian Girberts Jr. They are good people. What could they possibly have done to you?

Chief Edwards: Do, you remember the trial of Brian Girbert who raped a murdered a 17-year-old girl?

Jim Carson: All charges were dropped. That young girl was a tcase, and she consented to everything. She was drinking before and after the party. No one knows what happened to her when she left him. She was also into doing drugs.

Chief Edwards: That young girl was my daughter. So, I am going to give you a chance to come clean about everything. You will answer all my questions truthfully, and at the end I may let you live.

Jim Carson: How, do I know you won't kill me after I tfter I tell you everything you want to know?

Chief Edwards: You don't.

Jim Carson: I told you everything I know.

Chief Edwards: Dr. Seibi was he killed because of his research and his cure for diseases?

Jim Carson: We couldn't let that get out, it would have crippled the Pharmeuatical industry. We would have lost trillions of dollars. People would have stopped seeking medical attention from doctors, clinics, and hospitals. People would have started looking into alternative medicines.

Chief Edwards: He had to go. Is that why people who find out the truth end up dead?

Jim Carson:: Did you really come here to ask me this? Does it matter who we killed or why? Just know this. If they had a cure that we didn't approve, then they had to die. They had to go if they tried to uplift a race minority, or fight for a cause we didn't approve of

Chief Edwards: Why did you lie under oath about being with Brian Girbert after the party? Then when the video of you raping her, killing her, and dumping the body came out you buried it. No, one reported, investigated, or even wanted to hear about the video. When I went to the police, they told me that they would get right on it.

Jim Carson: The Girbert family are a part of the G.O.D.S, and they are very powerful people. Even if I would have denied being with him, they would have found someone else to vouch for him. They had judges, cops, reports, politicians, and whomever they wanted on their payroll. Your daughter was at the wrong place at the wrong time. Sorry.

Ring..Ring... Ring

Chief Edwards: Hold on I have a call.

John Sr : Hello Chief Edwards

Chief Edwards: I have him. Do we still have a deal?

John Sr: Yes, you want me to let you all live in exchange for killing Jim Carson.

Chief Edwards: If, I take him to my News Station I can have him on every single change all around the world in minutes. They will know that you all are cloning and open the door to many more questions.

John Sr: Yes, we have a deal. How is my grandson doing? Is he will his wife and kids?

Chief Edwards: Don't worry about then, they are all safe. We stopped you from putting up the towers, we destroyed your warehouse, and we are prepared for whatever else is to come.

John Sr: I like your spirit Chief Edwards: Always the optimistic. You have the same get up and fight attitude as my son and grandson. Put me on speak phone.

Chief Edwards: You are now on speaker phone; he can hear you.

John Sr: Hello Jim, it seems that you have gotten yourself in a bit of a mess. Jim as you well know you have been replaced by a clone. Your wife knows and kids know. Everyone has come to terms with it, and so shall you. Even if you find a way to get a meeting with the group you will be dead by the end of that day. I have the final say, and I say that you are a liability.

Jim Carson: I didn't tell them anything?

John Sr: Of course, I know you didn't tell them anything. You told them everything. However, no one person knows everything. So, if you tell them about plan A, B, and C, then we will just move to plan D.

Chief Edwards: Why go through all of this? You are killing off your own people, and for what? This New World Order will only create even more chaos. People will never bow down to your hate group.

John Sr: We are not a hate group. We are above any love or hate. We are the chosen ones from God himself. So, we live in his likeness, and rule as such. He made us to lead the strong into the Promise Land and seen the weak to the Heavens.

Chief Edwards: You killed your son and his wife. You are shot your grandson, framed him for 4 murders. How can you live yourself? You are just as bad as they are.

John Sr: The world is a very dark place. You people walk through life with blinders on. No, one sees, or wants to see the truth for what it really is. All he had to do was follow my rules, but he had to be a hero. Every single hero has fallen. You are either with us, or die being against us. He made his choice, so now he must suffer the consequences of his actions.

Chief Edwards: Whats do you have planned next? Tell me whats going to happen from here, or I swear go public.

John Sr: Go, public. We control the world, and there isn't anyone you can go to that cannot be brought. Your story would be buried or discredited before you could even get one view. I tell you what I want you to know. You all are still alive because we allow you all to live. You cannot defeat us, but I commend you all for trying. However, we have grown tired of your antics, and we will be putting it end to it very soon.

Chief Edwards: What's do you have planned next? Tell me what's going to happen from here, or I swear I will go public!

Chief Edwards: We agreed that my friends would live in exchange for Jim Carson. You cannot go back on your word. You said you were a man of your word.

John Sr: Yes, I did, and I will keep my word. However, the other members want my Grandson out of the picture. This I cannot promise and is out of my hands. As, for the rest of you, I can promise that you will get to live in our New World Order.

Jim Carson: I can still fix this John. Just let me fix this!!!

John Sr: There isn't anything to fix. Make peace with the G.O.D.S for we are sending you to the Heavens for your service is no longer needed. There's nowhere to run, there's nowhere to hide. We are always with you my peace be with you as you become one with the earth.

Jim Carson: Hang up!!!

Click...

Chief Edwards: What have you done? We had a deal, and now you have ruin everything. How do I get in contact with him?

Jim Carson: He was never giving to keep his word, and he was never going to let me back into the organization. I just realized what he meant by I am always with them, and I will be sent to Heaven. They gave me the cure, or a pro-type of the cure.

Chief Edwards: How, do you know that? Why would they give you the cure? Wouldn't you know if they gave it to you? You are a software and tech guy. So, wouldn't you know?

Jim Carson: I was in an accident a few months ago, and I was in a bad car accident. My wife told me that I had been drinking and I told my driver to take the night off. It was late and it was raining, and I crashed the car coming from a Pub. I don't remember any of this. What I do remember is meeting with my team earlier that day at one of my warehouses. I woke up, and with my arm wrapped in a cast. My wife told me I lost a lot of blood and was in a coma for about a week. They must have put the implant inside of me, and now have reason to active it.

Chief Edwards: So, my friends are in danger? They know where they are?

Jim Carson: I don't think so. When your people were taking me to their secret location, they had a device that scanning me. One of the guys put this device around my neck and covered my face. I think they had a device jamming its tracking signal. The Ministers place is probably secured as well as this vehicle, but I think as soon as I step out I am dead.

Chief Edwards: Well, where is the chip located

Jim Carson: It is in my arm. We will have to make it back to the site, but that will be a problem. They will have roadblocks and checking every vehicle for me now.

Chief Edwards: So, what's the plan?

Back at John Sr office where he is planning his next move.

John Sr: Did we have a location on Chief Edwards and Phil Yates?

Surveillance Agent: No, Sir. They are jamming our signals. Our satellites can't pick them up, and the trace on the phone has them in New Zealand.

John Sr: I know their location to active the chip in his arm? He can't go public with our plans. Find them, or you all are dead!!!!

Ring…Ring..Ring..

Pam: Hello John my love.

John Sr: Hello my Queen. Where you able to take care of our little problem?

Pam: Yes, everything is going according to plan. How are things going on your end?

John Sr: Phil Yates hasn't been located yet, but not a problem. The next phase of our plan is a go.

Pam: Have you located our grandson?

John Sr: He, still under the impression that he can save the world. C

John Sr: He, still under the impression that he can save the world. Chief Edwards wants to play let's make a deal. So, I humored him into thinking that if he gave us Phil Yates that they will all live.

Pam: We, need John Jr. To take the fall, or people will start asking a lot of questions.

John Sr: He, will come out of hiding soon enough. When he does come out, he will go to jail for what we have done.

Pam: I have already contacted people on the inside to make sure he doesn't live to tell his side of the story.

John Sr: I brought your favorite red wine that has been aging for over 100 years. We must celebrate tonight.

Pam: We can't celebrate until the final phase is done.

John Sr: By the time you arrive dinner will be ready, and our problems will be solved.

Pam: I am sure they will be my love. I have another call. I will see you soon.

Russian G.O.D.S. Member: Is everything going as planned?

Pam: Yes, everything is going according to planned.

Russian G.O.D.S: The other members are starting to doubt you and your husband leadership.

Pam: We help build this organization into what it is today. Without us you all would have been lost. Remember who you are talking to and know your place.

Russian G.O.D.S: Sorry your Goddess. No, disrespect. Your President seems to be cracking under pressure, and people are starting to rebel against the lockdown your country has put in place.

Pam: We have planned for every scenario. What is happening we knew would happen. We have everything under control. Tell the other members not to worry, and don't call me again unless its urgent.

Russian G.O.D.S Member: Yes, my Goddess. My apologize. Goodbye.

Click...

Back at The Ministers Secret Hide Out. I turn onto the News.

Let's see if anything is happening on the news

World News: It is April 27$^{th}$ and States are slowly starting to open their cities. The Illinois Governor has a fight on his has as a Republican Representative went to court to block his stay at home extension. Most states should reopen May 1$^{st}$, which is a few days again. It has people wonder with the death toll rising from this virus is that a wise decision. What's more important the lives of the American people or the economy? I am Thomas Thompson for World News.

So, they want to reopen the states, but why? We still don't know what's going to happen. It appears every time we stop one of their plans, they have another one/

Mr. Blackmen: Then, we will just have to stop their next plan, and the plan after that. Kid, no one said this was going to be easy. We just must concentrate on winning the war. Each battle is going to be harder than the next. Do, I hope we win each battle? Yes, I do. But I am being realistic. I just want to stop them from destroying the world. We may not be able to save everyone, but at least we could try to say as many as humanly possible. Hold on my phone is ringing.

Ring..Ring..Ring

Chief Edward: Don't talk just listen. We don't have that much time. I am brining Jim Carson back. We need to get the implant chip out of his arm, we can study it, and use it as evidence against them. I will put us on speaker.

Jim Carson: Hello, this is Jim. John your Grandfather will have you killed once you get inside the prison. Even if you happen to by some miracle avoid prison, he will make your death look like a suicide. For their plans to continue working someone must take the fall for them. While everyone is looking at you, they will be onto the next phase of their plan.

The Mentor: I thought you told us everything. So, what is it that you haven't told us? Why should we believe you? This could just be a desperate attempt to save your life.

Pastor: I am happy that you didn't sell your soul Chief Edwards. A lot of people would have gone through with it after what you have been through.

Chief Edwards: I am not proud of what I have done, but I can't undo what I have done. The only thing I can do now is to continue to move forward. Do we someone that can remove the chip?

The Mentor: I will have a team in the Medical Unit set up and ready by the time you both get here. Come back in the same way you left. Don't stop for anyone. Take the back roads, and Chief Edwards radio silence until you get here.

So, what's the plan?

Mr. Blackmen: We wait.

About an hour pass, and the security calls The Minister.

The Mentor: They are here. They are in the garage. Phil Yates is being taken the the Surgery room, and we will see Chief Edwards in the Board room.

We all had to the board room. Chief Edwards is sitting in the room.

Chief Edwards: I could explain.

Mr. Blackmen: No, need to explain. You did what you had to do. So, now we move on.

Yeah, no judgement here. We must move forward. Did Phil say what their next plan was?

Chief Edwards: I was able to talk to your Grandfather and get some new information from Phil.

What did my Grandfather have to say?

Chief Edwards: He told me that we are in a losing battle, and they

NORMAN AMOS SIMMONS JR.

are allowing us to live. Everything up until now has been a part of their master plan. Fear is what they are spreading, and we are doing a damn good job at it too.

Pastor: Once all the evidence comes out, then the America people wouldn't be afraid anymore.

The Mentor: Its, more to the story isn't it Chief Edwards?

Chief Edwards: Jim Carson has the virus inside of him, he was the first to get the cure. Once injected they will be able to kill each person by using their satellites as well as their towers. They are rebuilding all the towers as we speak. Those vaccines we destroyed were all just testing kits. They are going to blame John Jr., and said he was working against the American people. You will be labeled as a trader and wanting to profit from the spreading of the virus.

How would I profit by killing millions of people? I hope proof my family is alive and well. I also was with Mr. Blackmen at the time Robert Farmsworth body was found.

Chief Edwards: They hacked your email, phone records, and computer. You now have blueprints, invoices, text messages, email, and pictures of you sacrificing animals at a cult retreat.

The Mentor: They got the chip out of Phil's arm, and he is ok. They are studying it now. We should find out what all it can do in a few hours. Until then Phil Yates will be in the interrogation room.

Jim Carson comes into the interrogation room and we have him on speaker.

Jim Carson: Thank you for saving my life and allowing me to help you guys. I cannot change what I have done. I know you all see me as a monster, but I want to change that. I want to help take them down. All I am asking for is a chance to prove myself.

Chief Edwards: Now, is your chance, so tell us what they are planning to do next. No, more lies.

Jim Carson: Destroying the vaccines, tearing down the towers and kidnapping me was all a part of their plan. However, what they didn't plan was for me to get the implant out and join you guys. They wanted you guys to think that you had won and have you all gone back to your normal lives. When John Jr. Finally goes home, he will be arrested on site. The Chief, Blackmen, Minister, and the Pastor are going to be killed.

Pastor: So, their plan is to kill us, use the towers and implants to depopulate the earth as they first had planned?

Jim Carson: Yes, and no. That's just part of their plan. If you look at the State of the America, it is divided. If you push hard enough society will start pushing one another. The President is one of them and he will use this to fear to keep himself in office.

Jim Carson: Children will be home schooled, colleges will be online, most businesses will stay closed, the stock market will start seeing a decline, and eventually this will cause our country to wage war from within. Martial Law will no matter at this point, and out of know where the government will come with a cure to save the day. People will take the cure by choice, the numbers of death reported will go down. The stock market will rise, employment rate will rise. Then with a push of a button people will die, and it will be because of the second wave of the virus/ They will say that this strain was even stronger than the one before.

Mr. Blackmen: So, how do we stop them?

The Mentor: We, can't. Fear is a powerful thing. If you put the fear in someone, it is impossible to make them see anything but what they are afraid of. So, we must show them that we are not afraid. We will continue to tear down the towers, destroy the vaccines, and make it public. Give them something to believe in.

Jim Carson: I can help with that. If we flood the air waves with powerful messages. Show the people that you all will not stand for this, then maybe we will destroy the fear. When the cure is ready, they will not hesitate to activate it. They are already bleeding society dry of every penny it has. Once they worked all the essential workers to death, they will kill them. They are putting your people on containment ventilators, beds, and giving them test kits that have all been exposed to the virus. Even if you don't show the systems of the virus, they will say you have it. When people die in the hospital now, it will be because of the virus to increase the fear.

So, where do we start?

The Mentor: We go public and tell the people to fight back. Show them videos of the towers going down. Let them see the warehouse carrying the cure that was designed to kill them. If, they want a fight let's give them one. Our people need to see them for what they are, and that's cowards.

I cannot step foot off this site. Once a camera or the authorities see me, I will be put in jail. Once in jail I am as good as dead.

Pastor: We can use this to our advantage. We will have someone go live when the put you in handcuffs. You tell them you have been framed, and then while you are in jail, we will upload the evidence. Once it's on social media, it is out there for the world to see. They won't be able to stop it once it gets out there.

Couldn't I just go back to Africa, and upload it from there? I am all for saving the world. However, I don't want to be selfish by taking my wife's husband, and my daughters' father away from them. I must think about them as well.

Chief Edwards: No, one can make this decision, but you. You have made it this far, so it's up to you if you want to keep going. Regardless what you decide, they are coming for you Kids. They will not stop until you are framed for murder, trying to take over the world, and depopulating the world.

Jim Carson: Have every news station, your tuber, blogger, wannabe reporter, and anyone with a camera phone at the police station. Turn yourself in and tell them you are innocent. Have every civil rights activist, and influential person speaking on your behalf. Once you start trending you will become untouchable.

No, ones untouchable.

Jim Carson: People aren't going to listen unless you all make them listen. Let me make this right. President Dumpsters supports want the states to reopen to go against the government and some of your people just are tired of being treated like prisoners. Eventually Dumpsters supports are going to blame the minorities, and the minorities are going.

All this is going to start is a race war and no one wins.

Jim Carson: : Push back with a vengeance. This will give the Dumpster administration a reason to force the cure on everyone. They don't care if his supporter dies just if your people die with them.

Pastor: So, it settled we will leave first thing in the morning. I will call my people and have them meet us in front of City Hall. We will have the NAACP, Rainbow Push, and every black advocate in the state coming out to support you. Trust me this will work, and because of the lockdown wouldn't even see a day in jail. They may just drop all the chargers once the evidence gets posted to social media.

Mr. Blackmen: No, offense Pastor but let's leave the reporting to the professional shall we. Chief and I will call our connections. We will have the entire world watching this. This is bigger than him or us. They are using us as the first domino to depopulate the world, and once we fall the rest of the world will fall right with us.

Chief Edwards: Blackmen is right. Let us handle putting the word out there. You can still get everyone you know to join us and help us take them down. We are going to need all the help we can get. I know a few people at our company that would love an opportunity to do some good for a change. We must do this right because one wrong me, and they won. Losing is not an option.

The Mentor: You all have a valid point and must do what you feel is right. I will stay behind and see if I can find out other options. We must be prepared for the worst-case scenario.

I am prepared to see this through all the way no matter what.

The Mentor: My People victory is upon us, yet defeat is in the air. Let's not fear the unknown for my God has bestowed upon me what is needed to defeat the devil in any battle. So, lets fight for not ourselves, but for the very survival of our people.

So, we will leave first thing in the morning.

Everyone leaves and goes to their room. I call my wife and let her know what's going on. This may be the last time I talk to her for a while.

Ring..Ring..Ring

Tiffany: Hello my Love

Hello my Queen. We came up with a plan. I am turning myself in, and I am going need for you to send a copy of the video you made to all the guys here, and to people you trust. Just in case something goes wrong; I want the truth to come out. I love you and my girls.

Tiffany: I love you as well my King. I am proud of you. Your parents would be proud as well. I know that they are watching you from Heaven. Don't worry about what may happen. God has already put a victory in front of you. All you must do know is work towards it. We love you to. Remember we are with you every step of the way my Love. By for now.

Bye for now my Queen.

Click.

I closed my eyes and before I could go into a deep sleep there was a knock on my door. It's Mr. Blackmen and Chief Edwards. What time is it?

Mr. Blackmen: It's time for us to eat breakfast, and then head on out. You can't change the world on an empty stomach.

Chief Edwards: Everyone's in the dining hall. We called everyone and everything is set. City Hall will have the whole world watching. History is about to be made.

We are all in the dining hall eating. Even Phil Yates is here with us. Its funny how things can change within 24 hours.

Jim Carson: Thank you for giving me another chance. When we take them done, I will make sure that I be a voice for change. I want to start helping people and using my white privilege to help make the world a better place.

Mr. Blackmen: It will take more than a day for us to believe you. Trust is earned Phil, and something I don't just give away.

Pastor: Well, I think what you are doing is very courageous. You could have given up or found a way to take us out. Instead you are here helping us take down your former organization. So, I say thank you, and I look forward to seeing your new journey ahead. I will take John and Phil Yates to City Hall. John we can pray on our way there. We need all the help we can get.

Chief Edwards: Since the Minister is staying that just leave me with Mr. Blackmen. I guess you are riding with me Mr. Blackmen.

Mr Blackmen: Love you to Boss. Let's hit the road people and lets change the world.

So, we leave The Ministers secret base, and in two cars. I am travelling with Phil Yates, and the Pastor. Chief Edwards and Mr. Blackmen are riding together. The time has come for me to stand up for what I believe in. I am so glad God brought me to this point and with these amazing men.

Jim Carson: Don't worry about a thing John. You are in good hands.

Pastor: Yeah, John the Lord works in mysterious ways. This

could be a blessing in disguise.

How so?

Pastor: He brought us all together for a reason. Nothing happens by mistake. Everything happens for a reason. We are here to show Gods people the way.

You are staying to sound a lot like my Grandparents.

Jim Carson: : So, when we get their John, I am going to need you to tell the world what they are trying to hide. Let the world know that a secret organization hell bent on destroying the world exist.

Pastor: Hello, yes, we will be there soon. Yes, he is with me.

Was that Chief Edwards and Mr. Blackmen?

Pastor: What? Oh, yes that was them. They were just wondering where we were.

Why would they be wondering where we were; they are right in front of us. Wait, where did they go?

Jim Carson: Pastor, I think you may have made a wrong turn somewhere.

Pastor: I think you're right.

I text Mr. Blackmen and he text me back. Where are you?

Ring..Ring..Ring

Hello. I think the Pastor made a wrong turn. I think he's lost.

Mr. Blackmen: You guys were right behind us. How did he get lost, and he was right behind us?

Chief Edwards: Tell them just follow their GPS, and it should get them back to the main to City Hall.

Pastor do you have your GPS on? Chief Edwards said just put in City Hall and it will take us straight there.

Pastor: I know where I am at now. Tell them we will be there shortly.

Mr. Blackmen: I can here you. We are almost there. If you run into any trouble call us back.

Jim Carson: ; Sure, thing .

Click...

I started texting Mr. Blackmen

I think something is wrong. I have a bad feeling.

Mr. Blackmen: (I agree. There is something strange going on. Turn on your 360 app, and I will be able to track you. Don't turn your phone off. I don't think they were planning to come to City Hall.)

What are you saying?

Mr. Blackmen: (I think they are both working for your Grandparents)

If my signal drops, I want you to tell my wife and kids that I love them. Tell them I tried and that I will always be with them.

Mr. Blackmen: (You will have the chance to tell them yourself. If they are in a deadzone, then we will find you. You couldn't have made it that far. The tracker says you are heading south. We are literally 20 minutes away from your location.)

Pastor: I think he knows Phi.

Jim Carson: I see you texting, so we will just let the cat out of the bag. The Pastor and I are both member of the G.O.D.S. Well I am still a member of the organization.

Pastor: I was a member of the G.O.D.S way before I was a member of the Ancient Protectors. Why do you think I have been able to stay connected to everyone and everything? I am doing Gods will, and through his will I am given the power to place judgement on the undeserving.

What about your clone taking your place and them wanting to

kill you? So, the chip in your arm was a fake?

Jim Carson: You are a very smart young man. Too bad you aren't going to live long enough to tell your story. See, we have perfected cloning, but we only use it when it is deemed necessary. We knew that you guys wouldn't have trusted me unless you thought I was be replaced. The clone you saw is just a stand in for when we need him. I bring him out when we have intel about groups trying to assassinate me, or if we need him to be a decoy. He is my own personal insurance policy. I have 3 clones of myself at my disposal.

Where are you taking me?

Pastor: We will reunite you with your family.

How could you do this? You were like a father to me.

Pastor: You should have listened to your Grandparents. All you had to do was follow G.O.D.S Plan. You had to be your father's son, so you will have to pay for the consequences of your actions.

Jim Carson: Kid you have a lot to learn about the world. Everything is smoke and mirror. It's the slide of the hand. We are literally in plain sight, but no one sees us. Lies are more important than facts or the truth. I wasn't lying about you going to jail, and you will help change the world. We are here. Phone please.

I handed Jim Carson my phone. I looked outside the window of the car. There are 4 Federal agents outside with two black SUVs. We are on a ranch in the middle of nowhere. I can see nothing, but corn for miles. I refused to get out of the vehicle and the Pastor pulls out a gun out of the glove compartment.

Pastor: Move. Let's go.

Jim Carson: Your Grandparents are waiting for you inside.

I walk inside the house and in the kitchen is my Grandfather.

Grandfather: Come in and have a sit. Join me in the kitchen so we can talk.

Where's your wife? I thought this was going to be a family reunion.

Grandfather: She couldn't make it, but she sends her love.

Of course. She's probably out buying me and I love you grandson card.

Grandfather: Enough with the small talk. If you want answers, ask now.

Why, are you doing this? What's the purpose of all of this?

Grandfather: You, and your Dad are a lot alike. I should have known you wouldn't be able to handle this blessing bestowed upon you. This was a gift literally from the G.O.D.S. You and your father saw this as a burden. These people are mere mortals, peasant, and weak. The blood of the G.O.D.S are pumping through your veins.

So, you had the Pastor turn his back on his people, his faith, and the church?

Grandfather: He is doing what God created him to do. The Pastor is of greatness, and your people are beneath him. Doing the G.O.D.S work from the church has awakened so many of our worshippers who will do anything to be in the presence of the divine.

So, Jim Carson vaccines, chip implants, and warehouse was all just a distraction?

Grandfather: Everything that has been told to you has some truth to it. You see we need the world to depopulate. Since Americans like free will we wanted to let them think they had it. The rest of the members are doing what is needed to depopulate their people of their country. However, America must pretend as though it's a democracy ran by a President. If we could just kill of most of the population, we would have done it a long time ago.

So, what's going to happen to American and the rest of the world?

Grandfather: Don't worried about them, it's you that should be thinking how I will survive day one in a prison where people will know you tried to kill of most of the population. These are men with wives, kids, and family members. Do you think they are going to let you survive the night?

My friends are going to make sure I make it, and you will go down for all you have done.

Grandfather: Oh, yeah right. You are talking about the evidence you have against us. Well, that will never see the light of day. Even if it did who would believe you, or stand up against us? We are connected to everyone and everything in this world.

My wife is going to send the proof she's alive to the authorities, and the media.

Grandfather: By the time it gets to a judge, or someone who may not work for us you will be dead. Even if this reached mainstreamed America it will be buried so deep in social media no one will care for years. This pandemic we have created has just begun. Your people, the President's people and those in between are making this so easy for you. We literally can just sit back and watch the planet destroy itself. We will just wait it out and take out the trash when you all finish killing one another.

Chief Edwards and Mr. Blackmen will be here soon with the police.

Grandfather: No. They will be meeting my lovely wife and her team of mercenaries. Chief Edwards and Mr. Blackmen couldn't be brought or bribed. We tried to threaten them to join, we even tried to have them kill you years ago. They did not cave, and I commend them for that. The Pastor kept an eye on the both. I told you my son, we are always watching.

So, this all about destroying the world. Why would you want to kill most of the population?

Grandfather: Most countries are overpopulated. Just think

about it there would be less crime, poverty, hunger, diseases, greed, and death if there were less people in this world. No, one wants to be the bad guy. Everyone wants to see the glass as half full. Imagine a world free of violence, hate, struggle, and pain. We are going to start a new world, and make it a place where we could live in peace.

So, you will have blood on your hands while preaching peace on earth. Save me the we are the world speech. I don't buy this I want to save the world act. So, why are you really doing this?

Grandfather: You are so blinded by fear that you can't see the truth. Therefore, your people and the people all around the world could never survive what's to come. Every culture and way of life is different. But one thing always stays the say, and that's fear. People will always use fear as that common element linking you all together. This link will bridge the culture gap killing you all.

You will not win. I will fight until my last breath. I will make it out of there alive. When this is over your organization will pay for killing and infecting millions of people with this virus.

The Pastor and Jim Carson walks into the kitchen as my Grandfather prepares his beef stew.

Grandfather: Jim Carson, is everything ready?

Jim Carson: Yes, everything is ready as planned. We have already reached over a million infected in the US only. They are really pushing for the cure to be mandatory.

The Pastor: I have been spreading the word that God and prayer is the cure. They need to follow social distancing isn't what God intended. They all believe that God will save them all. So, if the go to the hospital the ventilators are infected with the virus. They will die from spreading the virus or receiving the cure.

Grandfather: It looks we win either way.

You all are sick. I promise you that you will not get away with this.

The Pastor: Still fighting until the end I see. You are blinded by the hope that your people will rise and unite. Don't think for a second that you can change the world. There are 3 black men in here, but only one thinks he is above us all. Just because you have the need to be a hero doesn't give you the right to think we are beneath you. We are doing to to  save lives. What will you do when the food, water, land, and natural resources run out?

The Pastor: Would you be able to make the tough calls? Would you be able to decide who lives and who dies? Yes, they want to kill off most of our people, but that's better than killing us all. Who do you think, they will come after when the world starts crumbling? We will be the first to go. Don't give me that we would unite. The first sign of chaos, and we will turn on one another.

Jim Carson: He tried. At least I can give him that much. Do, you know why your people always loses? I will tell you why, and it's not only because of the color of your skin. Its not only because of what you can do, it's mainly because what you all hold onto. Your people always hope for a better day.

Jim Carson: Hope is what kills your people and pushes us ahead. See, my people know that we must step on the backs of others to get to the top. We learned that a long long time ago. We don't step on one another. We find a group, race, or ethnicity and make them carry the weight of the world on their shoulders. Your people built this country, and we are just taking everything back. We gave you all a fighting chance, and you blew it. So, now we have to say goodbye.

Grandfather: Do you know how much Medicaid, Medicare, and HMO are costing hospitals? They are paying more of out of pocket cost, than they are seeing profits. So, by killing off those first who has no income, low income, or need government assistance will help revitalize a dying economy. Their sacrifices will not have been in vain. It's time to eat. I can't send you always on an empty stomach. Now, what type of Grandfather would I be if I do that to you?

I don't want nothing from you. Just kill me now and get it over with.

Pastor: They will kill you soon enough in prison don't you worry. It is all a part of G.O.D.S Plan.

The tv screen has an incoming call. My Grandmother appears on the screen.

Grandfather: Hello my Love. Is it done?

Grandmother: Hello my King. I see you have John Jr. There. I am sorry I couldn't make the family get together. We seem to have ran into a bit of a problem.

Grandfather: What happened?

Grandmother: It seems like they have help that we didn't know about. There was a group of Black soldiers that ambushed us. Chief Edwards and Blackmen got away.

Grandfather: Who were they? Were they the Black Tigers, African Coalition, The Kingdom., or Black Generation, or the Ancient Protectors.

Grandmother: I don't know maybe you can ask John Jr. Who they were? Don't think for a second Kid that you have won anything. This changes nothing.

I told you Grandfather that you weren't going to win, so do what you have to do. We will keep fighting. I don't know who they were, and I wouldn't tell you if I did.

Grandfather: Get him out of here. I am sick of looking at him. Enjoy you last day on earth. Your sacrifice will not go unnoticed. The G.O.D.S thank you.

Grandmother: May your blood feed the earth and bring new life to those who have been chosen to worship us.

Both of you go to Hell!!

Jim Carson and The Pastor grabs my arm and takes me to the SUV. The Federal Agents puts the handcuffs on me. I get into the back sit, and the Pastor shuts the door. As the vehicle drove away; I could see them both looking at me. They were proud of what, they had done to me. I arrive at the Federal Prison. No, reporters, no social media, and no one there to fight for me. I am happy that my friends got away, but I am afraid it is too late. After being processed, stripped searched, fingerprints, mug shot, and pushed into the shower I felt defeated.

Prison Guard Muhammad: You will be sharing a cell with Quran Mohammad. Don't worry no one will touch you. You are under our protection now.

The prison guard leaves and goes into his office down the hall.

Quran Mohammad: I am Quran Mohammad: I am a brother of The Nation. I was told if you made it here, then you were going to need our protection.

Quran Mohammad: This entire wing is of The Kingdom. . The guards, the residence, and even the medical staff are of The Kingdom. The cell block below us is the Black Tigers. The cell block above is are the Ancient Protectors. So, don't you worry you have protection up high, and down below.

So, why are all of you here? It just seems strange that they would put you all together knowing how powerful you all are.

Quran Mohammad: They wanted to divide us all and ship us down sate. Each one of us was framed for crimes we didn't commit. We stood up against injustice, got intel that they didn't want us to know, or found out ways to unite our people put us here. See, they want to continue to see us divided. As, long as we are killing one another, then we will never be a threat. They don't fear us; we fear us.

So, you don't think they are worried about us uniting?

Quran Mohammad: The Kingdom , The Ancient Protectors,

and the Black Tigers to this very day preaches that. Do you seem people uniting? We unite only when its trending or it's the popular thing to do at that moment. I am all for people rebelling against the man and the government. However, going to kickbacks, house parties, and giving the devil what they want isn't smart. They created a virus to kill us, and we are spreading it like wildfire.

So, you don't really believe that there's an actual virus out there? I was told that it was fear that was the virus, and the cure will be forced on us to finish the job.

Quran Mohammad: Yes, I know who you are. You are the grandson of John Sr. The Leader of the G.O.D.S. He wanted you here to take the fall for murdering Robert Farmsworth, creating this virus, and killing off millions of people all around the world. In a few days they will open the America back up, so they can create havoc all around the world. They want the rest of the world to think it's over, so they can depopulate the rest of the world.

So, how do we stop them?

Quran Mohammad: I talked with The Minister. Chief Edwards and Mr. Blackmen made it back. They had a few bruises, but nothing serious. The video of your wife and kids is being uploaded on social media, to every official we could trust. You will be out by sunrise. They will not stop coming for you. So, be ready for what's to come.

What about you and everyone else here? There must be something I can do to help you all get out of here.

Quran Mohammad: Don't worry about us. We will be out in due time. There is a war coming, and we will be right there beside you when the time comes. Get some sleep you have a big day ahead of you.

It's now May 1$^{st}$ and there is a knock on the cell bars.

Officer Muhammad: Looks like you only had to spend one night here. You are free to go, and your property will be in Out Processing. There is also a couple of guys waiting for you at the front gate. Keep your head up, Allah will see you through this, and remember you are always being watched. I will give you a minute to get yourself together. I will be down the hall when you are ready. Just call for me.

Officer Muhammad walks away, and Quran Mohammad gets up to shake my hand.

Quran Mohammad: You are free from this prison, but in order to truly be free you must free yourself from the hold that society has on you. You are mentally, physically and spiritually imprisoned. Until you can break the shackles that you have on you, then they will continue to win.

Thank you for everything my brother.

Quran: Wa-Alaikum – Salaam

Alaikum –Salaam.

Officer Muhammad I am ready.

Officer Muhammad escorts me to Out Processing, and the White Brotherhood looks at me as I pass their cell block. Some of them are making death hand gestures as if they were cutting my throat. One guy yells out "My brothers will be waiting for you on the outside. What side noose do you were?"

Officer Muhammad: Now, that you get your 3 months in the hole my brother. Don't mine them. Keep walking and do what needs to be done.

I make it out of Out Processing and to the front Gate. Chief Edwards and Mr. Blackmen is waiting for me. There are 3 SUV with them outside with them.

Mr.Blackmen: The Mentor called in backup. We need to move now if we are going to get where we need to go.

Are we going back to The Mentor's hideout?

Chief Edwards: Were not going back to that one. That particular site has been compromised. I am sure the Pastor told them the location. The Mentor deleted all his files and cleared it out before they could get there.

Mr. Blackmen: So, even if they can get inside everything is gone. He also left them a little partying gift. It is rigged with explosive, so whoever gets inside won't make it out.

That's good to know, so what happened to you guys? My Grandmother said you guys got away.

Chief Edwards: These guys helped us get away. This vehicle has a tracking device on it that only The Mentor can locate. It also has cameras, microphones, and its bullet proof. These guys belong to the Black Movement Society, which is part of multiple groups such as the Kingdom, Black Tiger , African Coalition, Black Generation, and the Ancient Protectors, and countless other groups all around the world.

Did we beat them? Were you able to upload all the evidence?

Chief Edwards: The internet has been shut down since yesterday. Every internet provider whether its local or a big corporation has been shut down by the Department of Homeland Security. They are saying that there was a security breach, so until further notice there will be little to no internet access.

They are trying to silence us; they don't want the truth to come out. All their talk about how they own everyone, but they are afraid for the world to see them for they truly are. Is there any way to get me on the News?

Mr. Blackmen: I think for now, its best that we regroup. Get to The Minister safe, and sound.

Is my wife and kids still in Uganda?

Mr. Blackmen: Yes, and she is better off staying put for now. I don't know how we missed the signs. The Pastor of all people are with those monsters. He preached the word of God but is following them devils. On top of that we were tricked by Phil Yates.

Chief Edwards: We all were fooled, but now it is time for us to move on. There is nothing we can do about the past, so let's make sure we are ready for what's to come.

So, we arrive at The Mentor's Mansion, and the gates open. There are guns all around the perimeter. Mr. Blackmen, Chief Edwards, and I are escorted inside. Our escort waits outside in the SUV's. The three of us are in his meeting room. There are 5 people already inside, and then walks in The Mentor..

The Mentor: Hello my fellow brothers. I brought you all here today. Because we are at war. Now, they want to prey on the simple fact that we are all divided. They want to use the hate we have for ourselves, our skin color, and for one another to win this war. I don't know about you, but I am not willing to let that happen. So, I am asking you what are you all willing to do to see our people victorious?

I will them all to pay for what they have done. They are trying to silence us, divide us, and wipe us from existence.

The Mentor: It's good to see you again. They wanted you dead, but my God has other plans. They wanted you out the way, but I tell you God said not today. They want you to run and hide, but my God says to fear no man for he will protect you as you walk through the darkness.

What is the plan?

The Mentor: I want you to meet The President of the Black Tigers, The President of Black Generation, The President of the African Coalition, and The President of the Ancient Protectors.. We are the Black Movement Society, and now so are all of you. This is bigger than us, and it's about to get worse.

President of the Black Tigers: John Jr. Your mother is my little sister, and I am your uncle. After her death I left Chicago, and I reconnected with all the Tigers around the world. We will get through this. I am sorry that we didn't meet under better circumstances, but I had to stay away to keep you safe. They have been watching our moments for decades.

The President of The Ancient Protectors: As you all know the Pastor was a spy for the G.O.D.S. We knew that we had a mole, but we could never had imagined it would be him. The infected toll is over a million in America alone, and a million people have been reported to have recovered from this virus. All around the world But I have a feeling that somethings not right. Things aren't adding up.

He only managed to steal some classified files, but only one was damaging. We had contingency plans if someone ever tried to infiltrate our organization. Even though he was one of our top members, he still had little access. However, he was able to get a hold of a list of our operatives' that were undercover in their organization. I am afraid since the internet went down; they are their own.

The President of Black Generation: We are here to protect our brothers and sisters. Whatever you need I will make sure that you get it. I have intel that the G.O.D.S have a new plan and it's called Project X. No one knows exactly what it is, but once it released its fatal.

The African Coalition: This pandemic is nothing, but a smoke screen. We must find out what Project X is and put an end to their tyranny. Stopping them from releasing Project X will cripple them. They have tried to kill us off one by one. Now, they want to destroy us all together once and for all. We can't let that happen. No, we will not let that happen!

The Mentor: Their President is opening the country back up. Everyone think this pandemic is over, the alarms are no longer sounding. People are ignoring the results. Unemployment is at an all-time high. Corporations are getting bailouts, but not required to bring their employees Martial Law has been lifted, and people are free to roam the streets. We don't know if what's going around is their virus, or it's the common flu. What I do know is we must treat this like an act of war. We are at war my people. Some of us may not make it to the end, but we will see this through to the end.

A soldier of the Kingdom walks into the room, and whispers something in The Mentor ear. He turns on the tv in the room.

The Mentor: I think you all should see this.

World News: President Dumpster: I am the President of These United States, and I am proud to inform you that we have won against this virus. The cases of death have gone down tremendously. I have done what most President that came before me were afraid to do. The former President didn't act in time to stop this virus, but I stepped in. When people were too afraid to act, I stepped in.

President Dumpster: My team and this administration have done an amazing job and the numbers will prove it. Even though the fake news will not give us create I think the American people know the truth. So, people go back to work, go back to the restaurants, gyms, theaters, and play some golf. I think we are also considering reopening the schools this fall, but for now they will stay close. Everything else will be open. Go on a vacation you all some time off. You fought your way out of a pandemic. Don't forget to vote for the man that saved your lives this fall. Thank you.

The Mentor: So, America and the rest of the world is back open. I spoke with other world leaders. There will be limited travel all around the world, but for the most part its business as usually. He is putting the economy before the American people. There hasn't been no cure, vaccinations, or plan to stop this pandemic. So, the question is what's Project X?

Whatever it is we can't let it leave Chicago. It starts and end with us.

President of the Black Tigers: How do we even know if it's not a group of cities, states or even countries that are included in this Project X? For all we know this could be yet another trick or distraction.

President of Black Generations: He's right we must find out what Project X is soon before the world goes back out into a world going down in flames. They want us all to die. People will start killing each other because now we are truly on our own. We must show them that's it's a better way.

What about the rest of the world? If we are going to change the world, we must do it together. So, we are going to have to reach out to other community and world leaders. They want to keep us all divided us all divided, and it's working. I am all for saying my people, but not at the expense of other races downfall.

The Mentor: You are your parents' son. No, one is saying that we must step on the backs of others to make it out of this alive. What we must do is make sure that our people make it out as well. I am not going to sacrifice my people lives to save anyone else. I don't expect any other race to do the same for my people. By, saying our people we stop the destruction on the rest of the world. This war starts and ends with us.

Mr. Blackmen: If they are limiting access to the internet, then we cannot prove to the world that they exist. The more time is waste, it will get even harder to prove to the world that they exist.

Chief Edwards: I just got off the phone with some of my contacts in Italy, and they told me not to drink the water. They were told that the water supply will help cleanse the world.

The Mentor: So, how reliable is your source? Can you trust them? We have always been two steps behind them. If they can poison the water supply, then the world as we know it is over. Millions of people all around the world will die.

The President of the Ancient Protectors: It will stop the world as we know it. Why would they contaminate the world, it hurts them as well? If the poison the world, then they will not have access to clean water as well. Animals, plant life, and even the air that we breath will be affected. This doesn't make any sense.

The President of Black Tigers: If this is Project X, then there must be an end game. What do they gain by destroying the water supply all around the world. Do they have an antidote?

The President of Black Generation: Maybe it only affects human. IF they perfected a virus that only attacks the immunes systems of human could be the reason why they chose to poison the water. The water supply is quick and easy to give it to the entire water. It may not kill everyone, but it will kill off majority of the population.

So, if they created a virus to put into the water supply that only kills human, then how do we stop it?

Mr. Blackmen: We must prove it and expose it to the world. Even if we can't take their organization down, we can stop them from playing God.

When does Project X supposed to be released?

Chief Edwards Italy believes it will happen on May 5$^{th}$. Blackmen see if you can reach our friends in Mexico, and see if they heard anything about Project X.

Mr. Blackmen: On it Chief.

The President of the Ancient Protectors: So, they want to kill the world on the Day of the Dead. They want to seize the day. If all of this is true, then how do we stop them? Cinco De Mayo is in 4 days.

If they are going to do it Jim Carson and the Pastor will be involved somehow. We find them, and I believe we will find Project X.

Mr. Blackmen: Chief Mexico has closed their country off to the outside world, and they have shut off their water supply until further notice.

The Mentor: I will call the other members and see what it is they know. Until then we do nothing, say nothing, and stay together until this is over. We are going to put it end to this once and for all. My security will show you all to your rooms. Get some rest. We will continue this first thing in the morning.

As., We were all leave the room, and The Minister turns on his tv and the group that attended the meeting in Uganda were on the screen in their countries.

In the Mentor conference room:

The Mentor: Thank you all for joining me on such short notice. There has been a new development in the next phase of the G.O.D.S plans to depopulate the world. We have been told by a reliable source that they are planning on poisoning the water supply all around the world.

President of Italy: Yes, we were aware of that. I had one of my Delegates contact Chief Edwards. My men that were undercover in their organization were killed not before sending me a file called Project X. Project X is their end game. They want to put a deadly virus in the water that only kills human beings. They are also the only ones with an antidote if one of them gets infected. My country and most of the other countries as well has shut of their water supply until this is over.

China Delegate: What are your people planning on doing about this? The other Delegate was a spy for them, and most likely told them who we are. I have no more agents to help you defeat them. Because of you I must cut off anymore communication with your country. We are no longer apart of your cause. You all are on your own.

Russian: Putin has made it clear that those that oppose this will be killed. You shouldn't have let those two spies go. They were able give them intel on the agent you had working to take down the G.O.D.S. We are now going inside blind. So, we can no longer help you all in this fight. You are on your own.

United Kingdom: We must do what is in the best interest of our people and I suggest that you all do the same. Stop them from getting the virus into your water supply. Until this is over all communication will be cut off. We were barely able to use our Satellite without them knowing. Our internet access is very limited, so I will make this quick. Good luck and may God be with you all.

Uganda President: Sorry Mentor, but I will have to agree with everyone else. I am with you all the way my brother, but this fight you will have to fight alone. Stop them were you are, and we will stop them from destroy our people over here. We are in this together. Our God be with you.

Keyan Delegate: I don't know if we can win this battle but trust me we will win the war. Don't give up, but we must protect our people at home. I hope you understand that this is not us turning our backs on you. We are not divided, it's the total opposite. This has brought us closer together, and when this is over, we will make them all pay. I promise you my brother, they will pay for all they have done.

I was standing by the door listening. One by one each country said they couldn't or wouldn't help take the G.O.D.S done. One by one their boxes with their faces went dark until their where no one left.

The Mentor: You can come back in John.

Sorry I didn't mean to listen in.

The Mentor: Everyone is closing their borders and shutting off their water supply. Their President will not allow us to shut off the water supply in every state in America. So, we must find out how, when, and where? Get some sleep. I will see you in the morning.

So, I left The Mentor's in the room. I get to my room, and my wife is calling me.

Ring..Ring..Ring

Tiffany: Hello my King.

Hello my Love. Is everything Ok?

Tiffany: We are at your family's place.

What happened? I thought they were going to let you all stay there.

Tiffany: They fear what's coming. So, they sent me and the girls back. I guess it doesn't help that the person who master-minded the destruction of the human race is your Grandfather.

Well, I am glad you're back. I am not sure what to say, but I think we can stop them once and for all this time. I love you and my girls. I will see you soon my Queen.

Tiffany: I will see you soon my love. Be safe. Bye for now.

Bye for now.

Click.

I am not sure if I happy she's back in Illinois. This changes everything. Do I go home and be with my family, or do I continue to push forward? Tiffany would want me to stop at nothing to do what I felt was right. She would be right here with me if she didn't have the girls with her. So, I will keep going to make sure they are safe, and the rest of the world.

It is morning time and its May 2, 2020. We have 3 day before Project X is released. Everyone is in the conference room, and I am the last one in.

The Mentor: I spoke to the world leaders, and they have confirmed that Project X is indeed what we thought it was. The G.O.D.S are planning to depopulate the world by putting a deadly virus that only kills humans. However, we are on our own. They are going to protect their people and the lives of their country. So, now we must protect every single American even the ones that wants us dead.

Chief Edwards: It gets worse. Turn on the News.

The Mentor turns on the tv and World News comes on. World News: Hello I am President Dumpster of the United States of America. We have opened back our country, and we want to celebrate the lives of the livinging as well as the dead. So, please join me on May 5$^{th}$ as we are having an Air and Water Show saluting the men and women that have been risking their lives during the pandemic that has recently died out because of the tremendous job that I have been doing as President. We will also be remembering the lives of those that are no longer with us celebrating their legacy they left behind. I am asking each country, state, and city to dye their water white and fill it with white rose petals. So, I want each pond, lake, river, ocean, and any body of water you can find showing their support. Those that refuse to do this obviously doesn't care about their people like I do. So, I think this is a good idea. No, other President cares about the people as much as I do. The people of the United States want this and need this. They asked me to do something special for them, and I think this is the best idea anyone has ever came up with. Don't forget to cast your vote for me this fall.

The President of the Black Tigers: This idiot loves to hear himself talk. So, now we know how they plan to release Project X. They are going to use The Air and Water Tribute to poison all water supply. How are we going to stop them from dying all the water? We will also have to somehow do it for every single state and territory of the United States in 3 days.

There must be a company that they all will be using. We find the company and we can stop them.

Mr. Blackmen: Kid, there could take days or even weeks to just track down all the companies Illinois are using let alone the rest of the country.

Couldn't we just get all the mayors, governors, alderman's and state officials in one room? We must at least give them a fighting chance. If we show them the proof that we have maybe they will just call the whole thing off.

Chief Edwards: Its worth a shot.

The Mentor: I will make some calls and see if I could get every-one in one room we must make this happen by May 4$^{th}$.

Chief Edwards: I still have people that owe me a few favors, so we can have them all meet here if that's ok with you Minister.

The Mentor: Yes, I will just say it's a party to bring us all to-gether. This will be our only shot, so we must make it count.

The President of the Ancient Protectors: I will make some calls as well. We need to make sure that this doesn't get out as anything other than a dinner party.

The President of Black Generation: We will make sure that they all make it here safely. I will make sure this doesn't get out. I have family, friends, and members all around the world that I need to protect. So, whatever you need we are here to do what we can. I will make sure that every single state official I know gets here.

The President of the Black Tigers: You can count on us as well. It is time the world knows how powerful we all are united. Every-one will make it here safely and this will end before it even gets started. They will not win this war.

Everyone leaves the room to make some calls and prepare for the meeting that will happen on May 4$^{th}$ a day before Project X is scheduled to be released.

Its May 4$^{th}$ 2020, and everyone is arriving to The Mentor Mansion. He opens his banquet hall that can seat over 200 people. It is set up like an actual diner party. There must be over a 100 people in this room. Every important person from each city, state, and territory is here. The people of the Black Movement So-ciety are at the first table in the front and the table for Illinois are to the right of them. The Minister gets up in front of the crowd of guest to speak on the stage.

The Mentor: I wanted to thank each one of you for coming

out today. This country has been through dark day and as we continue to move forward, we hope to see the light of day. I brought you all here to let you all know that in one day a group of terrorists will poison every water supply all around the world. You can make sure calls and check with the other questions to confirm. The Air and Water Tribute is nothing more than a distraction to put the virus into the water. Now, you don't have to believe me, but if you let the Tribute happen, then you all will be putting your people at risk. This virus is a deadly virus and they're isn't a cure. I will now have John Jr. Come up to speak.

Hello, I am not sure if you all know who I am. I am the grandson of John Smith Sr. We have limited access to the internet, and there hasn't been much said about the pandemic since May 1st. Now suddenly, the President wants to pay a tribute by dying the water. There hasn't been any proof that the virus is gone, so what's the rush with a tribute? China, Africa, Italy, and the list goes on how all shut off their water supply.

All we need to do is stop them from dying the water, and having the tribute take place. Have someone check the tanks of dye, the planes, and the people operating them. If I am wrong, then you can arrest me afterwards for lying.

Mayor of Chicago: We could at least make some calls and if he is lying then we put him in jail. However, if he is telling the truth, then he just saved our country.

Governor of Illinois: I agree with the Mayor. Let's makes some call right now and see what we can come up with. I don't think anyone should leave this room until we get to the bottom of this.

Mayor of Atlanta: I don't think we should talk to the press about this until we have all the facts. Whomever we call, they must keep this private. If word gets out, and this is true we could cause them to do it today.

The Mayor of New York: I just called my friends in Italy and the told me that its true. I agree with the Kid. We can't let this tribute happen. My city is out, and I suggest you all do the same.

Mayor of Chicago. Chicago is out.

Governor of Illinois: Illinois is out

Mayor of Atlanta: Atlanta is out.

One by one every single state, city, and territory of the United all called cancel their tribute. They turned the internet back on so the world could witness our destruction. However, instead they saw each state decline the President offer to show tribute for reason that they believe that the Pandemic isn't over.

I shook everyone's hand to thank them for doing the right thing. This was a proud moment in history that the world will never know happened.

The guest that we invited all leaves the mansion to go back home. We stopped the G.O.D.S. The men who were driving the truck filled with dye were hired by a person they said they had never met. They paid them in cash no questioned as to fill every single water supply in the United States with poisonous dye. The pilots of the planes that were supposed to be in the tribute were mercenaries hired to spray poison over the water and the people. They all went to jail, but they don't know who hired them. There was no paper trail because they were given cash in a drop box.

Mr. Blackmen: We won kid. See, what happens when you don't give up? Now, since we let the cat out of the box everyone will be on high alert for now on. You made an impression on them, so when you call, they all will listen. I bet your Grandparents are some place crying right now. They lost and they know now that they can't beat us.

Chief Edwards: Small victories should be treated as such. Sure, we one this round, but I am sure there will be others. Maybe not today, or tomorrow. You did good Kid. Take care of yourself.

Where are you all going?

The President of the Black Tigers: I am going back home, but

I promise you I will come back to see my great nieces, and your wife. I must make sure that my people are ok, and I will be back.

The Mentor, you don't look happy about this.

The Mentor: Anytime I get to beat the devil at his own game is a victory. However, something doesn't add up.

What's wrong? We stopped them from putting the virus in the water and put those who tried in jail.

The Mentor: Yes, and there was no one on the other side trying to stop us. This was a little too easy.

If they plan something else, then will stop them when they do.

The Mentor: You're right Kid.. You will finally get to go home and spend some time with your family. Enjoy this moment. I am proud of you son.

Thank you.

As, I looked around everyone is gone, and I started to walk away. I can see The Mentor still seating at the table looking towards the stage. It looks as though he had something on his mind. I kept walking; maybe I should have turned back around. I had to get to my family.

One of the Kingdom members let me take his car, so I could go home to my family. I arrive to the lake house in the middle of no-where. My wife and kids run out to greet me.

I wake up and its now May 5th and there is no celebration, tribute, but the President is on the news.

World News: I am the President of the United States. I am appalled that someone would try to sabotage our great Tribute by poisoning it. Luckily, my team acted quickly in notifying the Department of Homeland Security about this. Therefore, we need the wall to go up, and to limit who we let inside our country. If I didn't put restriction during the pandemic, we would have had more people trying to kill us. I have protected our country better than any President in history has. You can check the statistics and it will show you that the American people feels safe with me than they have with any other president in the history of presidents. So, I am glad that I decided to cancel this event, and proud to say all the people behind this are behind bars.

Tiffany: Look at your President.

No, that's your President.

We both started laughing. My girls run into my arms and gives me big group hug.

My phone rings, and there is a knock at the door. Tiffany grabs a gift box with my name on it.

Ring.. Ring.. Ring

Hello, who is this?

Grandfather: Did you get your gift I sent you?

I don't want anything from you. I thought you and your wife would be out of the county by now since you couldn't start your New World Order. You lost and you will not destroy the world.

Grandfather: Who said I was going to destroy the world?

What are you talking about? Your tricks will not work on me. I trusted you. When I came back, I wanted to get to know my Grandfather, but instead I found out you're a monster. My Grandmother faked her death and helped kill my parents. So, this conversation is over. At least open your gift before you hang up the phone. Trust me.

Tiffany: It's a bottle of wine, and a thank you card.

Why are you giving me a bottle of wine and a thank you card?

Grandfather: The G.O.D.S would like to thank you for all you have. done for us.

I haven't done anything for you and your fellow monsters. We stopped your implants, towers, and manmade viruses, and now

Project X from depopulating the world. The people who tried to poison the water supply are all in jail, so Project X failed.

Grandfather: Who said Project X was about a deadly virus we were going to put into all the worlds water supply? Of course, it was us who spread that rumor. Project X was never about poisoning the water supply. We needed someone or something to be able to spread the deadly virus for us. We needed a carrier. Someone who wouldn't show systems but could spread the deadly virus by contact. This virus is airborne and anyone in this individual presence will get it. Now, we had to make it last. So, the survival rate is 3 months tops if you are in good health. If you are elderly, young, or have a preexisting condition then you may only have weeks to live.

You are lying

Tiffany: My love what's wrong?

Grandfather: John you are Project X, and you have infected and spread the virus all over the world.

How were you able to do this? You are lying?

Grandfather: When I shot you, I shot you will a bullet that had the virus inside of it. So, when it went into your blood stream you became a carrier of it. Now, we have the antidote for our people and members. However, the rest of the world that we need will get the cure, and other will get water injected into them. By, the time most people around the world fine out what's wrong with them it will be too late.

Tiffany: My Love what's wrong? What is he saying?

Grandfather: John, talk to your wife. Your wife and kids don't have that much time left.

How could you do this to my family, and to the world.

Grandfather: I told you to follow the rules, but you had to do things your way. You thought you were doing the right thing, so now you must suffer the consequences of your actions. I didn't kill your family; John you did.

Click.

Hello. Hello

I drop to my knees and cry. My wife and kids wrap their arms around me. Kids go to your room I have to talk to your mother. The kids leave and goes to their room.

Tiffany: What's wrong my Love.

My Queen what's wrong with you? You don't look too good.

Tiffany: I have been feeling a little lightheaded all day, but I am fine. What's going on?

My Grandfather told me that I am Project X and I am the carrier of the deadly virus. You are sick because of me. Our kids are infected because of me. I have infected the world and they only have 3 months to live.

Tiffany: This could be another trick by him.

We hear something fall to the floor of the girls' room. We both run to the room. Both girls are on the floor. We feel them and they are burning up.

> *Tiffany: I called the doctor, but they said he died of the virus last week. This can't be happening. I can't reach my organization.*

I will see if I can reach the Minister.

Ring..Ring..Ring.

The Mentor:: Hello John

My Grandfather told me that I am Project X and they put the virus inside of me.

The Mentor: I know John. After you left, I realized that things didn't add up. The people that we met in Uganda started calling me one by one telling me that they were all sick. They all had the same systems. I tested my blood, and I got the virus. Everyone that meet you after you got shot got the virus. They think that you are working with them and planned this with your Grandparents.

I didn't know. When I got shot, I lost a lot of blood. I passed out and ended up at the Lake House. When I woke up, they had me wrapped up. I didn't know I was infected. I would have isolated myself, put myself in a hospital. I didn't know!!!

The Mentor: I know son. I know, but this is going to get worse before it gets better. You are going to have to isolate yourself before you infect anyone else.

I must get help for my wife and my kids. I can't let them die.

The Mentor: They are the only ones with the antidote, and they will sell it to the highest bidder. They are going to watch our people die and kill each other.

What should I do?

The Mentor: Fight. Take care son. May Allah be with you.

Click.

Tiffany: I am going to lay down for a little bit.

Ok, my love I will fix this. I promise I will fix this.

Ring. Ring. Ring..

Grandfather: Hello John. What can I do for you?

I need you to save my wife and kids. I will do anything.

Grandfather: It's a little too late for that.

I can't lose my wife and kids. I will do anything you want. Whatever you want me to do I will do.

Grandfather: You already have, and now you will have to live with it for the rest of your life without them.

Click…

No!!!!!!!!!!!

I picked myself up and go live on social media.

Hi, I am John Jr, and I am Project X. I have been infected with a deadly virus. A secret organization called the G.O.D.S led by my Grandfather John Smith Sr. And his Wife. My wife and kid are in the other room dying.   I don't know what to do or who to turn to. I don't care what happens to me, but please don't let them die. Whoever is listening please send help. I am at 555 Chicago Blvd in the Gold Coast District Condominium unit #1. Please send help. Police Brutality will increase, people will take sides, and racism will smile. People will start hanging Black people from trees with nooses. Calling the cops with be white privilege secret weapon. Hate and racism will no longer hide in the shadows. They want a race war, but we can give the world the change it needs. They want us to kill one another. They want us to turn on one another, but I still have hope. I still believe in us, and I hope you all do too. I can hear the sirens behind me, the police are coming up the stairs now. No, matter what happens to me now. We are the difference for change. Black lives matters, so don't stop protesting. No justice. No peace.

The National Guard knocks down the door and starts yelling get down on the ground now!!! The Police Officers grabs me. They have their knees on my neck, and I am yelling I CAN'T BREATHE!!! The CDC are wearing hazmat suits. The CDC runs to my kids rom.

My kid's door is wide open, and my wife is holding both. She looks at me as they handcuff me with their knees in my back. I whisper on my last breath I love you my Queen, and she whispers back to me as she blows me a kiss "I love you more my King."